His arm around her was sure and strong.

McKenna had forgotten what it felt like for a man to hold her. Emotions she'd buried suddenly surfaced like a strong gust of wind that sweeps around a corner and takes you by surprise.

She went up on her toes, joining him in the kiss. It seemed to go on forever.

Parker released her. He stepped back, moving out of her personal space. His stare was steady and direct as she looked up at him. "I'm not going to apologize," he said. "I'm not sorry."

McKenna couldn't speak. Her lip trembled from contact with his. Was she sorry? She didn't know. She'd never expected Parker to kiss her. She'd never expected to enjoy it. But she had. She should be ready to date again, to find someone she could spend her life with.

But Parker?

He wasn't that man. Parker Fordum was the last man on earth that she could have any kind of relationship with.

Dear Reader,

Driving Route 66 from end to end has been a goal of mine since I was first enthralled by the exploits of the two fictional characters from the television program *Route 66*. (I was also intrigued by the car.) Writing is a way of getting to safely do all of the things you can imagine. And so I gave my adventure to McKenna and Parker.

In researching this book, I watched some of the old television episodes from *Route 66*. Just as Parker has done in my book, I was rediscovering the road and the stories encountered and especially the people that make life interesting. I hope you enjoy *Promises to Keep* and that you will have your own adventure.

As always, keep reading,

Shirley

HEARTWARMING

Promises to Keep

—

Shirley Hailstock

HARLEQUIN® HEARTWARMING™

Recycling programs
for this product may
not exist in your area.

ISBN-13: 978-0-373-36738-2

Promises to Keep

Copyright © 2015 by Shirley Hailstock

For questions and comments about the quality of this book,
please contact us at CustomerService@Harlequin.com.

Printed in U.S.A.

www.Harlequin.com

Shirley Hailstock began her writing life as a lover of reading. She likes nothing better than to find a quiet corner where she can get lost in a book, explore new worlds and visit places she never expected to see. As an author, she can not only visit those places, but she can be the heroine of her own stories. The author of over thirty novels and novellas, including her electronic editions, Shirley has received numerous awards, including the Waldenbooks Bestselling Romance Award and the *RT Book Reviews* Career Achievement Award. Shirley's books have appeared on BlackBoard, *Essence* and *Library Journal* bestseller lists. She is a past president of Romance Writers of America.

Books by Shirley Hailstock

Harlequin Heartwarming

Summer on Kendall Farm

To my editor Kathryn Lye,
for making my stories better.

CHAPTER ONE

WHAT SHE WAS about to do was strictly forbidden. McKenna Wellington knew it, but she was going to do it anyway.

She glanced at the aged and torn rule sign hanging on the wall. Turning it over, she reached for the master switch and forced it up. The lights over the track flared on. In a flash, midnight became high noon.

Looking up, she squinted at the brightness. The buzz of the halogen lamps coming to life sounded like a cavalcade of bees. The bleachers showed bright red seats, and the infield was ripe with Kentucky bluegrass. No cars graced the field—except hers. The fully restored red-and-white 1959 Corvette sat alone, a silent sentinel waiting for its driver in the surreal light.

Nothing was scheduled for testing. There

were no spectators, no officials with stop watches or pit crews.

She was alone.

McKenna, the lights, the car and the night.

The wind was strong, plastering her flight suit to her body, but it wasn't rugged enough to affect her test. Snapping her helmet over her shoulder-length brunette mane, she slid behind the wheel. She took a moment to admire the car, running her hand over the leather upholstery, caressing the steering wheel, taking in that new car smell and admiring the gleaming chrome hood ornament. It had taken her a year to restore the car and tonight was its first and only test run.

With her hands on the steering wheel, Marshall came unbidden to mind. This car, this drive, was her idea, but he'd supported it. They were going to do it together. But now that was not to be, would never be. Mist rose to her eyes. She blinked it away.

Marshall had been gone three years. She missed him, but she'd learned to fill the hours of her days until she no longer felt she would fall into melancholy and sudden bouts of tears. Guilt had racked her when she no longer thought of him first thing in the morning or last thing at night, when his features began to fade and she had to concentrate to bring them into focus.

McKenna shook herself, raising her chin and pushing the past behind her. She turned the key. The engine purred with only the slightest pressure from her foot. Her heart beat faster. Sweat coated her brow in anticipation of future speeds. Adrenaline pumped through her system. The car was her baby and she was taking it for a ride.

Pressing her foot down several times, she let gasoline pour through the intake valves. The dual exhausts kicked white smoke into the cool air. The sound was exhilarating. Anticipation, like a drug, flowed through her.

"Come on, baby," she said aloud. "It's show time."

McKenna threw the car into first gear and pressed the accelerator. The Corvette took off as if it had a tail wind, digging its tires into the track, spitting up dirt and debris. The car punched forward along the artificially lighted track and headed down the straightaway. She didn't feel so much as a shadow of a shimmy from the backfield. Pride swelled inside her. She couldn't remember ever feeling this way before.

She'd done it. She'd rebuilt a car and she was driving it. But not just any car. This was Marshall's car. A 1959 Corvette Stingray. No one had helped her. No one was there to lower the engine in place, slip a seat down on its frame, install a radio, put on a tire or polish the chrome grill. The car was hers, totally. She knew every nut and bolt in it, every quart of oil, washer fluid, belt, muffler and filter. Each one had her personal handprint on it. This was her first step toward an adventure and no one was going to keep her from doing it.

She pushed the car forward a toe at a time, shifting the gears with the precision of a choreographed dance. They smoothly slipped from one to the next. There was no grind, no crunch, just the polished perfection of timing and engineering. The car took its head and McKenna let it have it. The speedometer inched up until it reached

Mach 1. RPMs soared. Tires spun, keeping traction with the pavement. The night wind ripped over the windshield, whistling in the lamplight like a knife cutting a path through which she flew. And flight wasn't out of the question.

At the first curve, she banked high, easing into the turn but maintaining speed. She could kill herself if the slightest move wasn't exact. The Corvette performed to her touch, slinging her around the turn and sending her straight down the fairway. McKenna took a moment to smile before bringing her concentration back to her driving. She went on, executing test after test, seeing what the car could do and making sure it would perform as expected should a situation arise when she needed speed, maneuverability or just plain getaway power.

Satisfied, she headed back toward the track entrance. She entered slowly, cooling the car down as if it were a thoroughbred. Turning off the engine, she got out and closed the door, admiring the beauty of the vehicle as if it were a Greek god.

The lamp lights still buzzed above her.

McKenna walked around the Corvette, she couldn't quit staring at it. She stopped and a smile spread across her face. Suddenly she jumped up in the air, doing the splits as if she were a cheerleader. Her voice hollered to the empty bleachers.

And that's when the lights went out.

SUDDEN CHANGES DISORIENT most people. McKenna was still in the air when daylight was switched back into darkness. Her eyes didn't have time to adjust to the change. Unsure of where the ground was or how high in the air she had jumped, she came down hard. Her hands reached for the car to break her fall, but it was too far away. Her feet hit the ground, her knees bent, and her butt made contact with the unforgiving track. Pain rocketed through her from her knees to her eyelashes.

Just as quickly as they had gone out, the halogen lamps burst on again. The instant change blinded McKenna. She heard footsteps crunch on the track. Fear surged within her. Thoughts of getting to the car raced in her mind and despite the pain, she was on her feet, moving forward when she heard her name.

Pivoting toward the direction of the sound, she waited to see who was there.

"What are you doing here?" Sam Sherrod strode forward followed by Parker Fordum. Sam was the test track manager. He didn't live far from the place and looked at it as his personal property. Sam was in his late fifties and had been with the company McKenna owned since before she took total control when her husband, Marshall, passed.

Seeing Parker had McKenna gritting her teeth. What was he doing with Sam? Parker was an economics professor and had once been friends with Marshall. McKenna never took to him. While Sam knew cars inside and out, Parker recognized it only as a means of necessity to get from Point A to Point B.

"Are you all right?" Parker asked.

The question must have awakened McKenna's nerves, because suddenly every pain receptor in her body sprang to life reminding her of her fall.

"I'm fine," she said.

"What are you doing here?" Sam asked again. "I saw the lights and thought someone had broken in. The kids do that sometimes, but they never turn on the lights."

"Sorry, Sam. I wanted to ride around the track for a while."

Sam looked at the Corvette and then stared as if he'd been struck dumb. "Where did you get this?" His voice was breathless as he walked slowly, his steps matching the cadence of his words. He fully circled the car, peering at it as if he'd found the Holy Grail. "You're not planning to bring this model back, are you?" His tone was negative, but McKenna knew he wanted a positive reply.

"Sam, we make parts, not full cars," McKenna told him.

"I know," he said. "A car is only a…"

"Few parts," she finished for him. Sam always said that. He had it printed on a banner and attached to the bumper of his personal car.

"Where did you get this one?" Parker spoke, also staring at the car.

"I restored it," McKenna said proudly.

"It's a beauty." His eyes seemed fixed on

the car. McKenna knew he hadn't heard her actual words. He thought she meant she'd *had* it restored. So far no one really knew that she had done it herself and she wasn't about to go into explanations at this hour.

"My father had one of these," Sam said. "He loved that car almost as much as he loved my mother."

"I know just how he felt," McKenna said. "Marshall had a replica of this on his desk at home. He told me once that he wished he could drive it like the wind."

"Was that what you were doing tonight?" Parker glanced over at the track.

"Something like that," she said, dryly.

"You can, of course," Sam told her. "But I'd feel a lot better if you did it in the daylight. I don't want to have to scrape you off one of these walls."

"It was something I had to do, Sam. And I needed to do it alone."

"I understand," Sam replied. McKenna knew he did. She could hear it in his voice.

"You've got it out of your system now, so we won't expect a repeat performance,"

Parker stated. McKenna could hear his censure loud and clear.

"No. No repeat performance," she said, keeping her tone as level as possible.

The next time she drove the car it wouldn't be on a track, but a road.

The Mother Road.

ONE OF THE hardest lessons McKenna Wellington ever learned was to win the battle for friendship. Lydia, Sara and Adrienne were as close to her as sisters. She'd known Lydia and Adrienne since they'd all played in the same sandbox. Sara she'd met in college, but she fit into the group as if she'd always been a part of it. They had been there for each other during most of the joys and hardships of their lives, but they were also the worst critics to her creativity that anyone could choose. And though she loved them, she would not allow them to run her life.

For most of her thirty years McKenna Wellington had fallen in step with others. Whenever she tried to assert herself, there was always a reason for her to forsake her plans and comply with someone else's.

Well, she was done with life by committee. Life was too short for her to put off doing things until it was palatable to the group. Marshall's death had brought that realization home.

She'd allowed her friends to talk her out of moving to Alaska after college and to ditch her plan to make a fortune and then return to the mainland. When she wanted to invest money in an upstart computer software company, they'd convinced her she'd lose her bra. That company was now a worldwide multibillion dollar enterprise. Before she married, she wanted to buy a house. They'd been there to explain all the maintenance nightmares that could happen and how she was unprepared to cope with them. So she'd remained in her apartment. Only after marriage had she and Marsh bought a small three bedroom bungalow. Then, when the business exploded, a larger home in the Chicago suburbs where she resided now.

Well, not anymore.

If she kept that up, she'd die never having lived her own life. Now she was planning to go to California—her way.

"I never heard anything so silly," Sara stated, pushing her shoulders back and rising up to her full height of five feet, five inches. Placing a hand over her mouth, Sara began to laugh as if McKenna's announcement was a joke. "McKenna Wellington, have you finally lost your mind?" Lydia and Adrienne snickered.

McKenna closed her eyes and took a long breath, pulling her anger under control. She knew this would be her friends' reaction. They had long since given up on their dreams. So had McKenna until three years ago when the man she'd married and expected to spend her life with had suddenly died of a heart attack, leaving her behind. Marshall was only twenty-eight. He would never be twenty-nine.

It had taken a while for her to stabilize the business, deal with the grief and assure the employees that their jobs were secure. But she was stronger for it now. And her dreams had returned. Dreams she'd put on hold so long ago she was surprised the door locking them still had a key. Marshall's death opened that door. McKenna was going to act on her own dreams and no one, not even her friends—her best friends—were going to talk her out of them.

"My mind is completely intact, Sara. And I don't think this is funny." She stared across the car in her garage at her three friends. "I'm doing something I've always wanted to do. I'm telling you because you're my friends, but I am *not* asking for your consent or approval."

The group looked a little stunned. It was natural that they should. McKenna had never spoken this way before. But she wanted them to know up front that she was not accepting any criticism or attempts to dissuade her from her plan.

"McKenna, you can't be serious," Adrienne jumped in. "First you invite us to dinner. A wonderful dinner, I might add. You outdid yourself with the Lobster Newburg. It was superb." Lydia made a French gesture of kissing her fingers and saying ooh-la-la. "Then you bring us out here to the garage and show us this…this car." She pointed a finger at the Corvette as if it would bite her. "A car you say you built."

"This is not a secret," McKenna said. "You've all known for a year that I was building this car."

Sara's face screwed into a frown. She looked at Lydia Osbourne for help. "We didn't actually believe you when you said that," Lydia told her. "Selling auto parts doesn't qualify you to build an entire vehicle. Where would you learn how? We just thought it was your way of saying good-night or that you didn't want to do something we did."

McKenna scowled at her.

"You know," Lydia tried to cover. "Like when Margaret Mitchell told her friends she was going home to work on her novel."

"Well, it was true when Margaret said it and it's true for me." She turned toward the red and white 1959 Corvette and spread her arms with pride. "As you can see."

"McKenna, be reasonable," Sara stated. She always began her arguments with *be reasonable*. "You can't turn over the management of Marsh's company to that idiot George Hightower and run off on this hare-brained scheme." Sara was the only person who dared to call Marshall Wellington

"Marsh" to his face. Sara was Marshall's sister. It was through her that McKenna had met him. And, like family, she protected her brother's interests even after he was no longer alive to do it for himself. McKenna was also protecting Marshall's interest. She would never do anything to intentionally hurt the company. It was her livelihood, too.

"It wasn't just Marshall's company. My sweat, tears and several years of my life are embedded in the walls of that business."

McKenna and Marshall decided on the idea at the same time. Both loved cars and both had contacts in the automobile industry. It was McKenna who first broached the subject of starting a business to service vehicles, but Marshall jumped right in as if they were both of the same mind-set.

Marshall knew the economy affected car sales, but people were willing to buy more efficient cars in a bad economy. Those that didn't, took better care of the car they already owned. Their business, of a full line of automotive products sold to both retail outlets and the automotive industry, had taken off.

The business didn't just sustain them, it

turned them into millionaires. But when Marshall got into the high-end, custom-made conversions, the carriage trade lined up and the business's annual income became serious money.

"I didn't mean to imply that Marsh did it all himself," Sara was saying when McKenna's attention came back to her. McKenna gestured for her sister-in-law to stop talking.

"George Hightower is not an idiot. He's a capable manager and Marshall trusted him implicitly. So do I. George will keep things moving if he has to go out on the floor and run the machines himself." She paused, waiting for Sara to refute her statement. Sara looked as if she disagreed, but she remained quiet.

"Good. Then there's nothing to keep me from pursuing my dream. Marshall is gone and I'm free and single. I'm alone here and I want to do this before I die."

"You're not dying…" Sara said but then questioned, her expression changing to concern.

"We're all dying, Sara!" McKenna shouted. Fighting to quickly compose herself, she continued, her voice at its normal volume. "When Marshall died, I wanted to die, too. My life had been so much his life. Without him I didn't know what to do, but after I was running the company alone for a while, I felt the old me emerging."

McKenna looked at her friends, studying their faces. "You remember the old me, don't you? I used to be brave, yearning for new experiences. I loved Marshall, but he held me back."

"Held you back. How?" Sara challenged.

"He didn't mean to, Sara. And I let it happen." She said the words gently. "I was happy to run the house, take a backseat to his decisions. I was happy to do what he wanted. We planned to have children, but our efforts were focused on the factory. We started the business and settled in. It took all our time and energy. But he's gone now and I don't want to die thinking I shoulda, woulda, coulda followed my heart and I didn't. If I fail, at least I'll know I gave it a chance. Can't you understand that?"

For a moment it was quiet in the garage. Silently she pleaded for their understanding. Lydia, Sara and Adrienne all had different expressions. McKenna didn't know if they were reviewing the younger versions of themselves, the people they used to be when their dreams were fresh and new and the thought of not accomplishing them wasn't an option, or if they were judging her.

"You haven't said anything, Lydia," Sara prompted. "What do you think of McKenna's plan?"

Lydia Osbourne was McKenna's oldest friend. "I don't think you can make a trip like this alone," she said.

"There," Sara seized the comment as consent that Lydia was in her corner. "Lydia's right. What woman do you know who wants to drive from here to Los Angeles alone?"

"And on roads that are cracked, overgrown with weeds or so badly in need of repair they're essentially nonexistent," Adrienne said.

"You're not going to talk me out of this," McKenna said. "I've planned it for a year and I'm leaving in ten days."

"Ten days," Adrienne said. "This car may

not make it from here to California. That's got to be..."

"2,400 miles along Route 66," McKenna finished for her. "And I know every single part of this automobile. I have personally installed every part, every piece. I know what its purpose is and what it needs to keep it working properly. This car is better equipped for a road trip than anything any of you drive." Her comment was a challenge and she didn't care how they took it.

There were drawbacks, but McKenna didn't know what they were yet. She chalked that up to being part of the adventure.

"At least take someone with you," Lydia said.

"The car's only got two seats and no trunk to speak of," Sara observed. "Where are you going to stay and how can you even put one suitcase in this thing, let alone one for another person?"

"Only you would call a fully restored '59 Corvette a thing, Sara. I'm not planning on taking much. I want to travel the land the way the two guys on *Route 66* did it."

"I thought Route 66 was a road?" Lydia asked.

"A defunct road," Adrienne added.

"It's an old television series, with two guys traveling the roads, finding work where they could, and having a wonderful time," McKenna explained.

"I never heard of such a thing," Sara said.

"It was before our time, but I watched the reruns on *Nick at Nite*," McKenna said. She'd watched them while Marshall was ill. It played in the hospital and she felt as if those two guys had kept her sane during an insane time.

"Isn't that a children's television station?" Adrienne asked.

"During the day, but at night they play vintage programs. The guys were Buz and Tod and they were the hottest thing going during the late '60s. They traveled that road working and meeting people along the way."

"How would you know? You weren't even born then."

McKenna was tired of explaining herself. She was going and that should be that. "The internet," she finally said, unwilling to go into how much she had read on the subject, the books, songs, associations she'd joined, not to mention the two Disney movies surrounding that road that came out only a few years ago.

"All of this is because of some fifty-year-old television program? I cannot believe you," Sara said.

McKenna clenched her jaws. At this moment she could strangle Sara. She wanted her friends to approve of her trip, not plant doom in her head.

"Sara, the show was only part of the inspiration for the trip, but it's something I want to do. I'd forgotten about it until I started watching those reruns."

"Sara has a good point, McKenna," Lydia said. "Have you given this enough thought? There are hundreds of things that can go wrong on the road. And trying to work your way to LA. How long do you think this is going to take? And what about emergencies?"

"I'll deal with them. If I can build a car, I can certainly drive it."

Lydia looked the car over with the eye

of a teenage greaser. "It's very low to the ground. Those roads haven't been maintained in years, if ever. You're likely to have trouble with the muffler and oil."

"I can handle it."

"If you get someone to go with you, I'd feel better."

"How about you going with me?" she asked Lydia.

"What?" Lydia said. "I can't—"

"Why not?" McKenna interrupted. "What are you doing for the next few months?"

"I have a job."

Lydia was a dressmaker by profession. She had a shop attached to her house and Sara worked there, too. They mainly did wedding gowns and big-ticket dresses for wealthy clients.

"Sara can run it while you're gone. You have a staff of people who make and alter the dresses. You've been doing management and client relations for years. And you haven't had a vacation since I can remember."

"Wait a minute," Sara said. "You're not considering this?" she asked Lydia.

"Of course not. I can't just up and leave."

"Lydia, it'll be fun," McKenna said. "The two of us, the wind in our hair, a car that any man over thirty would drool over. Just think about it. The open road. No cares. No deadlines. No one screaming for your attention."

Lydia considered it for a moment. She walked around the car, checking inside at the upholstery and smallness of the interior.

"Fine," she said. "We'll be like Thelma and Louise."

"No, we won't," McKenna exclaimed, her eyebrows raised in protest. "The Grand Canyon is several hundred miles north of any part of Route 66."

"I was kidding," Lydia said.

McKenna's shoulders dropped. "Lydia, I've been thinking about this ever since Marshall died." She faced Sara and addressed her. "It's something I want to do. I have to do it. Don't burst my bubble now."

"I know you're slightly off your rocker," Lydia spoke up. "But it's good to give life a jolt once in a while, instead of waiting for it to do it to you."

"Now she's got it, too," Sara said. "You're both crazy."

"The car's only got two seats," McKenna pointed out, ignoring Sara. "We'll be traveling light and that means no men."

"But Tod and Buz had women. Why can't we have men? Thelma and Louise had men, too, only they killed them," Lydia said.

"I draw the line at murder, but pretty much everything else is fine with me." McKenna smiled.

Lydia and McKenna grinned at each other. And then they grinned at Sara and Adrienne. After a moment, they all burst into laughter.

CHAPTER TWO

TWO MORE DAYS, McKenna thought, leaving the store. The last thing she needed for the trip was a lightweight jacket. She'd found one that was warm, but not bulky. It was red and swung inside the bag she carried.

She stopped along Main Street to look in the window of a small boutique. A royal blue gown expertly displayed on a mannequin stood in the window. McKenna gasped at its beauty. She could see herself wearing it. If she was going to a ball, it would be perfect. But her car was small and now she had a passenger. There was no room for anything superfluous. Not even a gorgeous royal blue gown would fit into the single bag she was using for this trip.

Not to mention her plans didn't include any evening functions requiring such a dress. Turning away, McKenna wasn't expecting anyone to be so close to her. She ran directly into the massive chest of a man. Strong arms came out to steady her. The bag dropped to the ground as her fingers grabbed and found hefty biceps and held on.

"I am so sorry," she began, looking up at the man she'd walked into. "Parker!" He was the last person she expected or wanted to see.

"McKenna," he replied, letting her go.

"Excuse me. I should have been paying more attention."

He glanced at the blue ball gown. "Apparently you were."

She smiled quickly, only allowing her lips to widen and close. Parker Fordum had to be the most boring man in Chicago and the surrounding suburbs. McKenna had had run-ins with him in the past and did not want either a repeat of them or to spend more time in his company than was absolutely necessary.

"As neither of us is hurt, I'll say goodbye," she told him. She reached down and retrieved her bag, then moved to leave, but Parker stopped in front of her.

"I hear you're planning an adventure," he said.

"I am." She raised her brows, meeting his gaze, ready for the challenge she knew would be reflected there. She wasn't disappointed. She had to look up, as Parker stood a head taller than her five feet, five inches.

He was a good-looking man. She had to admit that. His eyes were piercing and at times they could be comforting. She'd seen him look at Lydia with happiness then changing to a soft warmth.

Reflecting his European ancestry, Parker had thick dark hair, a square jawline and features that commanded attention. His arms were long, extending from broad shoulders. Equally long were his strong legs. While she wouldn't call him athletic, Parker and Marshall often went skiing together and they had a regular Saturday morning basketball game. She didn't know who, if anyone, he played with now that Marshall was gone.

For all his attributes, college professor described him best, the phrase like a tattoo. In her presence, at least, that was the personality he showed. Granted it was also laced with hostility. She didn't blame him for that.

She was hostile to him, too. The two of them just didn't hit it off.

"California, by way of Route 66?" His voice interrupted her assessment of him.

"How did you know?" McKenna asked.

"How often do we have the female owner of an international automotive parts corporation restoring a Corvette in her garage and planning to drive it from here to the Pacific?"

"I suppose word is all over town about my trip."

"I don't think it made it to downtown Chicago, but the entire township of Woodbine Heights has had the privilege."

"Adrienne or Sara?"

"Sara." He nodded.

McKenna had no doubt her sister-in-law would be telling the tale, including her opinion of how harebrained the scheme was.

"Don't worry about what she says," Parker told her. "The idea of driving Route 66 is fascinating."

"You think so?" she asked. McKenna forced herself not to blink. Was this the real Parker Fordum she was talking to?

"Absolutely," he said.

McKenna looked at Parker to make sure he wasn't being facetious. She knew people could say one thing and mean another. But his appearance seemed to be genuine.

"I envy you."

"What?" McKenna couldn't be hearing the straitlaced, put-everything-into-a-box Professor Parker Fordum was envying her.

"Taking off for the wild unknown with only your wits as backup. It's a brave thing to do."

She was about to thank him, but his next words stopped her.

"And a foolhardy one."

"Excuse me?" McKenna pushed her hand through the plastic bag's handle. She should have known he was setting her up. Parker was always true to character. How could McKenna have thought for a moment he would agree with her motives? She was going and she didn't need or want Parker's opinion.

"Don't you understand who you are?"

"Of course I do." And she knew who she was not. She wasn't someone who was going to be talked out of what she wanted to do.

"You are the owner of a billion-dollar business. You are female."

"Thank you for noticing. I might have missed those two points, especially as I come out of the shower each day. And I don't care to hear any more from you."

McKenna moved to pass him. Again he blocked her path.

"If you were only going on a driving trip, I'd say hail and farewell."

"But…" she prompted.

"But you're planning to work your way to the coast, doing only what you can afford."

"Parker, I'm taking enough money with me to get me there. It's not like I'm planning to sleep in a field or cook over an open flame. And Jim Talbott is expecting me."

"That's good to hear, but what about the safety factor? The world isn't as safe as you might think."

Leave it to him to put everything on a nice neat little graph.

"I'm well aware of the dangers and I'll be careful to stay away from them."

"From kidnapping?"

"You think someone wants to kidnap me?"

"Why not? You're a wealthy woman. You'll only have Lydia as backup and she'll panic the first time she sees a bug, let alone someone bent on harming the two of you."

"What are you talking about?" The bag on her arm was getting heavy. She wanted to be gone. She and Parker had never agreed on anything. Sara may have told him her opinion, but McKenna was leaving in two days and nothing he could say would keep her from going.

"Even though this is a small town, your movements haven't been lost on the population. Especially with everyone knowing now about this trip. And a red-and-white '59 Corvette will be easy to spot. If some guy takes it into his head to subdue you and hold you for ransom, what could you do about it?"

"I'm not sure. Maybe I could use some of my self-defense training and slam him to the ground with a kick to the groin and a chop to the larynx. Or maybe I should bring you along as my personal bodyguard. The only problem with that is the car only has two seats and they're occupied." Her voice virtually oozed with sugar. "The trunk is

available but it isn't big enough for someone with shoulders as wide as yours, or legs
as long." She stepped around him. "See you
when I get back." To herself, she added, *but
preferably won't.*

BY MORNING, THOUGHTS of Parker weren't
McKenna's main concern. The call came
half an hour ago. Lydia had fallen and was
in Mercy Hospital.

McKenna turned into the parking lot. The
lights of an ambulance momentarily blinded
her. The car skidded to a stop next to a white
van. Slamming the car door, McKenna ran
to the hospital entrance. The revolving door
hampered her hurried efforts. Inside, she
rushed straight to the room number Adrienne had given her.

Parker Fordum came out of the door as
she reached it. McKenna stopped, frowned.
She did not want to physically run into him
a second time. She remembered his arms
around her, the feel of his hands as they
steadied her.

"McKenna," he said by way of greeting,
his head bowing in a curt nod.

"How is she?" McKenna felt obliged to ask.

"She's waiting for you." He nodded in the fashion of someone used to tipping a hat, but as long as McKenna had known Parker she'd never seen him wear one. He stepped around her and walked down the hall. McKenna watched him go, but he didn't turn to glance at her. She'd been dismissed as if she was one of his needy students. Impulsively, she wanted to stick her tongue out at him, but someone might see her and it was a childish act.

"Lydia, are you all right?" McKenna asked breathlessly when she entered her friend's room. Lydia lay in bed looking pale and drawn, although she smiled. Her right leg had a cast on it up to her knee.

"McKenna, I'm fine. I fell off the attic ladder. It was so stupid. I was getting down a case for the trip and my foot slipped. Both the case and I came crashing down."

"Are you going to be all right?"

"I'm okay now. The doctor says my leg will heal just fine." She smiled and McKenna thought Lydia was trying to put her at ease.

By her expression, Lydia must have thought she looked panicky.

"I'll be up and dancing again before you know it." Again Lydia smiled.

"Why didn't someone call me last night?"

"You couldn't have done anything. I was in surgery and then I was asleep from the anesthesia. I had Parker call you this morning."

"Adrienne called me."

"Maybe he got to her before you. And you know Adrienne. She's probably called everyone by now."

"Can I get you anything? Are you in any pain?"

"I could use another pillow."

McKenna pulled a pillow from an empty bed and lifted Lydia forward to put it behind her.

"That's much better."

McKenna settled into the chair next to the bed. Lydia's face looked less pale than it had when McKenna had first seen her against the white sheet.

"I'm not going to be able to go on the trip with you," Lydia said.

"Forget about the trip. You're going to need help when you get home."

"I'll have plenty of help at home. Other than Sara and Adrienne practicing their remedial nursing skills, Emory was here when I woke up."

Lydia had been on-again, off-again in love with Emory Woodson for as long as anyone could remember.

"I'm just sorry you're going to have to cancel." Lydia adjusted her pillows.

"Cancel," McKenna said. "I'm not going to cancel." The words had come out automatically, as if she were used to getting her way.

Even hearing that Lydia had fallen didn't make McKenna respond with talk of cancelling her trip. Lydia was going to be fine. And besides, McKenna had planned to go alone and only agreed to let Lydia come to satisfy their friends. She'd be alone again, but she *was* going.

"You've waited this long—"

"I'm not waiting any longer," McKenna interrupted.

"But I've gotten used to thinking of us both going. You know, Thelma and Louise."

"Sorry. I was going alone initially. I'll just go back to the original plan."

Lydia pushed herself up a little farther. "I knew you'd feel this way. Even though you'd never think of doing this if Marshall was still alive."

"Probably not. With Marshall we'd be involved in expanding the business. I don't want to spend thirty years inside a factory, developing newer and newer products, and never see the world."

"Why is that road so important to you?"

"It's not the road."

"It is," Lydia contradicted. "If it wasn't that road, would you take the highways or even fly? You want to take *that* car over *that* road."

McKenna stared at the wall behind Lydia for a while. "It's been a wish of mine for a long time. And Marshall's, too."

"Marshall never said anything about wanting to drive 2,400 miles, or wanting to drive that road."

McKenna refrained from telling her that

there were some things that husbands and wives shared that other people knew nothing about.

"Why do you think Marshall had that replica in his office?"

"He liked cars," Lydia replied.

McKenna shook her head. "He didn't just like cars. He *loved* cars. Loved everything about them—the smell of the oil, the sound of a perfectly pitched engine, the squeal of the tires against the road. Every year he couldn't wait for the new models. Even the new paint colors excited him."

"I know," Lydia said. "Marshall lived and breathed cars."

"I asked him once about the car. Why he had the replica on his desk."

"Did he say he wanted one, wanted to take it on a road trip?"

"Not in those words. He said it represented a dream. He wanted the freedom the car represented. Not that he regretted marrying me. I wasn't the tether holding him in place. It was the business. We had so much responsibility because of it, the welfare of our employees depended on us. He took that seriously and said driving away wasn't in his plans any longer."

"When was this?" Lydia's voice was soft. McKenna felt as if she was trying to protect her from the memory of things she and Marshall would never do.

"Shortly before he died. You remember the business was taking a slight hit. We'd begun the custom work and we were pouring a lot of financing into it."

Lydia nodded. "And then he was gone."

McKenna felt her eyes tear up. "And then he was gone."

"And you decided to fulfill his dream."

She smiled at Lydia, a genuine smile. "It wasn't just his dream, Lydia. It was mine, too. I didn't build that car in memory of my husband."

Lydia gave her a scant look.

"Well, not totally. Building it was my idea, only mine. It was a way to help me deal with Marshall's death, take my mind off everything. Once I started, it became me. I wanted to do it. I wanted to put all those pieces together and complete it. And I wanted to take it on the road. Men aren't the only ones who think taking off into the wild is their birth-right."

Lydia held her hand and squeezed it. Then she released it. "I'm sorry that I can't go with you now."

"Don't worry. I'll have no problem being on my own."

"Well…you won't be going alone, actually"

McKenna raised her brows, curious. "I won't?"

"Parker is going to accompany you."

McKenna couldn't believe her ears. "Parker!" She almost screamed. "Parker Fordum?" She stood up and took a step back. "You've got to be kidding." McKenna's stomach churned at the thought of Parker sitting next to her in the small car.

"McKenna, Fordum is on sabbatical. He's a perfect replacement," Lydia said.

"Lydia, he's *old*, has no imagination and he wants to label and define everyone into a neat, little box. That's not the kind of person I am or the kind of trip I'm going on."

"He's not that old. He's younger than you are."

"That's not what I mean. He acts old, set

in his ways. He's too much of a by-the-book person. He would never fit into the way I want this trip to be."

"McKenna, he's not like that at all. Parker is a warm, funny individual who loves adventure. Give him a chance."

McKenna was shaking her head before Lydia had finished speaking.

"You can't go alone. It's too long a drive and too dangerous. And Parker could help out if the car breaks down."

"Is he a mechanic? Does he know the first thing about a car, about a '59 Corvette, other than how to drive one? And it has a standard transmission. Can he even drive a stick?"

"You still need someone to help you," Lydia insisted.

"No, I don't," McKenna said. She was sorry she'd ever mentioned the trip to her friends. Maybe it would have been better if she'd just called them from the open road and told them she was off and would be back when the adventure was over. She sighed. It was too late for that now.

"I don't need his help. I built that car. If it breaks down, I can fix it."

"McKenna, I'm not doubting your intelligence, but you might just need someone with strength to help you along."

"Lydia, it's more than that. You and I are women. The whole dynamic changes with a man. We can't stay in the same hotel room, so that means more expenses. I'm not familiar with his habits, his likes and dislikes in food, his pet peeves. You and I had agreed to eat simple, healthy food and to exercise everyday so we wouldn't get run-down or develop any health problems. I rarely even talk to Parker other than sharing a polite conversation at a party." She'd always cut short or avoided conversation with him altogether. And then there was the matter of Marshall and Parker.

"Then you two can spend the time getting to know each other." Lydia put her hand up when McKenna began to speak. "He's already agreed to spend part of his sabbatical on the road with you, so don't mess this up. You don't leave for two days. You'll have time to get used to the idea."

"What idea?"

McKenna turned to find Parker Fordum in

the doorway, holding a bouquet of flowers in a glass vase. She stiffened at his unexpected presence, then forced herself to relax. While she and Parker were like oil and water, he and Lydia had been friends since their college days. McKenna usually tried to be at the other end of the room whenever they were at the same event. She couldn't imagine spending weeks on the road with him. *Alone*.

"The idea of traveling a long distance with you," Lydia responded truthfully.

McKenna wanted to glare at Lydia, but she transferred her attention to Parker and said, "I was a little surprised when Lydia told me you agreed to stand in for her on our trip."

"She's very persuasive." His voice was almost a drawl, yet McKenna knew he'd spent his entire life in and around Chicago.

So he didn't want to go, she thought. McKenna took a step forward, coming up against the bed. "She tells me you're on sabbatical. I bet you're trying to finish a book. I wouldn't dream of taking you away from that. I know how proud you are of the books you write. And you probably have a deadline to meet. I can complete my trip alone. That was my plan from the very beginning."

"The book's done," he said. It sounded like a dismissal. "I have some editing to do. I can do that in the car when I'm not driving."

"And there's safety in numbers," Lydia chirped. "Since I can't go, McKenna, I'd feel so much better if I knew you were safe with Parker."

Safe with Parker, she thought. How could she be anything else. He was the epitome of boring. Yet McKenna felt trapped. She couldn't say what she really felt—that she'd rather spend the weeks having the hairs pulled out of her legs one by one than sitting in a car with Parker clicking away on a laptop as she chauffeured him from Chicago to Los Angeles. This was supposed to be a fun trip. It was her adventure. She didn't want it spoiled.

"I have my credit cards in case of an emergency. I'll be careful. Nothing will happen."

"That's not exactly true," Parker said.

McKenna clamped her back teeth together to keep from shouting at him.

"Other than the car breaking down, there are hundreds of things that can happen to a woman traveling alone."

McKenna groaned. "Not that eighteenth-century damsel in distress story? You're not my knight in shining armor."

"No, but I'm all you've got." His voice was stronger than McKenna had ever heard it. She stared at him as if he'd grown horns.

After a long moment, she glanced at Lydia. Her friend looked tired and McKenna felt guilty that the argument was contributing to her condition.

"Lydia, I have to go now. I'll be back later." The implication was she'd return when Parker was not in residence. Then she turned to Parker. "Can I see you outside?"

"McKenna," Lydia said, stopping her. "I'm so sorry."

"Oh, Lydia, you don't need to apologize. And if you want, I can postpone the trip," she told her, feeling true compassion for her friend.

"No. You've got your heart set on it. You're excited when you talk about it. Parker will be good company. You'll see." With that she gave a little wink.

Outside the door, McKenna turned to Parker. "I know Lydia's convinced you that I need a companion, but I assure you I don't."

"I was being truthful when I said there were a hundred things that could happen to you," Parker said.

"Those things can happen even if you're with me. So since the consequences are the same no matter the circumstance, I'd just as soon go alone."

"Have it your way. Just don't tell Lydia."

"Thanks, Parker." McKenna smiled. She couldn't believe her luck. She expected a heated argument, but he was being extremely reasonable. McKenna almost put her hand on his arm and squeezed it as a way of confirming her thank-you, but stopped herself before she did so. "Good luck with the book."

She walked away, her step a little lighter. McKenna didn't look back. She knew Parker was staring after her. Despite the way she felt about him, he made her conscious of her body. She was wearing jeans and a shirt, but she felt as if he could see right through her clothes.

The impulse to strut invaded her brain. She could give him a real image to keep when she was gone. Forcing herself to walk normally, her entire body was hot by the time she turned the corner leading to the elevator. She dropped her shoulders and took a deep breath.

"Thank God, I'm going alone," she said out loud.

She was disappointed that Lydia wouldn't be with her. Having a companion along had its advantages, but the idea of the open road and the freedom of doing whatever she pleased without anyone to censure her or question her decisions was exhilarating.

By the time McKenna reached her car, an idea was forming in her mind. All the arrangements were made for her mail, her bills, her house. She was practically packed. Since she would be traveling alone, why wait two days? She could begin her trip in the morning. The weather forecast was good for the next few days. All she needed to do was go to the bank and she'd be ready.

Her spirits rose in anticipation. Negotiating Chicago's traffic didn't even bother her today. By this time tomorrow, she'd be on some less traveled road and having the time of her life.

This was going to happen, she sang silently, drumming her fingers on the steering wheel as she made her way home. This was really going to happen. The open road, a vintage car and freedom. The old McKenna was out and the new McKenna Wellington was driving to Los Angeles, ready for whatever adventure awaited her.

CHAPTER THREE

Sunlight hadn't begun to paint the horizon when McKenna hit the button and the garage door started its upward trek. Her heart thumped. After three years of working, testing, searching for parts and finally getting everything to work in unison, she was beginning her journey today.

McKenna slid into the driver's seat and started the engine. The Corvette purred to life. Putting it in gear, she checked the mirrors and looked over her shoulder, ready to back out.

But her heart jumped into her throat and she stomped on the brake. The small car shrieked to a stop. McKenna threw it in Park and sprang out of the driver's seat.

"Parker Fordum, what the hell are you doing here?"

He sauntered toward her. Getting too

close and standing in her personal space, he looked down on her. "I thought you'd try something like this," he said.

"Something like what?"

"Like leaving ahead of schedule. Like disappearing without a word. Like getting your butt into more trouble than you can get out of."

"Well, who asked you to come along? I'm going by myself. Now get out of my way."

He stood in the middle of the driveway. McKenna went back to the car and got in the driver's seat. Before she could start the engine, Parker pulled up the passenger seat, dumped his duffle bag in the small space behind and climbed into the passenger seat.

"The car looks great." He smiled genuinely. "Will it ride as smoothly as it did in the '60s?"

Exasperated, she glanced behind her. His duffel bag used up more than the available space, pushing his seat slightly forward. And giving McKenna a view of his profile.

"Parker, get out. Go away. I don't need you."

"I'm going with you," he stated as if it was a foregone conclusion.

"No, you're not."

"I promised Lydia I'd take care of you. Now, you have two choices."

"Which are?"

"I weigh about 180. You can try to hoist me out of here and drive off alone." He dropped his chin and looked at her with a doubting-Thomas expression. "I doubt you can do that, even with all the ingenuity Lydia tells me you have. Or you can back out of this garage and head for LA with me. Your choice."

"Parker, we agreed yesterday that you were not coming with me."

"No, yesterday I decided not to argue the point. It wasn't going to make a difference, so why go through the effort."

"That's exactly why I don't want you with me."

"Because I don't argue?"

"Yes, and because you're not a companion. You're just someone taking up a seat."

For a long moment he said nothing. McKenna thought she'd gone too far. She didn't usually insult people. It wouldn't be good for business. And it wasn't her personality.

Finally he spoke, repeating, "You have two choices."

"I have one more choice," she said, pulling the key out of the ignition. "I can stay here."

He nodded. "That, too. But if you think you're going to wait me out, I've already thought of that. I'll park my SUV right in front of your garage. You can't get this baby…" He looked approvingly at the upholstery. "Out of the garage without me knowing it. So you might be able to outsmart me and leave some other way, but it won't be in this car." Again he looked at the Corvette, checking the back over his shoulder. "She is a beaut. If she drives as well as she looks, I take my hat off to you. Lydia told me you built it from the ground up."

"I'm not here to listen to your compliments." McKenna sighed and propped her elbow on the open window, resting her chin in her hand.

"What's it going to be? The road or breakfast? I'm hungry."

McKenna got out of the car and went through the laundry room door into the house. Rage surged through her, giving her an instant headache. This is not how she had planned to begin her trip. Excitement had soared through her system last night. It was difficult to fall asleep. Details of her impromptu plan had run through her mind like a relay team handing off a baton, one runner after another. When she did sleep her dreams were peppered with images of Parker and Marshall. And now here Parker was, in the flesh, making her crazy.

She stood in her kitchen feeling useless. What was she going to do? She could try waiting him out. He had to get tired of blocking her driveway soon. But the determination with which he'd said he was going told her he was serious. She could call the police and report him as a trespasser. She wasn't without friends on the force, but then Parker also had his contingent of buddies, too. One of the drawbacks of living in a small town.

She was going, she told herself decisively. This was her life and she wasn't going to let him spoil it. Turning quickly, she walked back to the garage. Parker was sitting where she'd left him, tapping away on a laptop computer. He'd apparently adjusted his duffel bag, since the seat now sat flush with the back of the car. His apparent nonchalance angered her further. He really was a stick in the mud and a stubborn one at that.

"All right," she said, holding back none of the venom from her voice. "You can go."

He didn't look up from his work.

"But there are rules."

"Rules?" He continued to focus on the screen.

"This is my trip and we go with my decisions. You don't question them and you don't try to overrule me. This is not a vacation and we're not a couple."

He nodded, still not looking at her. McKenna wanted to grab the computer from him and snap it closed. He was not going to spoil her plan, she told herself. She'd spent years building this car. She was ready. Every detail had been planned up to this day. From here to the end, it was life as it came. She hated to admit it, but Parker had now become part of the life *as it came* scheme.

Opening the door to the car, McKenna slid into her seat. Parker closed the laptop and turned to her. "I have some rules, too," he stated.

Surprised, she opened her mouth to say something, but before she could speak, he continued. "First, you will afford me the same respect that you would give to Lydia. You will talk to me with the same tone of voice that you would if she were here instead of me. I'm not going to go 2,400 miles fighting all the way. And don't..." He stopped her when she was again about to say something. "Don't tell me to stay here, because that's a decision that has already been made."

McKenna was taken aback. She'd never heard Parker speak with such force. Deep down it excited her to know he had a backbone somewhere. She'd always thought of him as weak and quiet, interested in nothing but being a dull college professor. Yet he really lived too well for that. At least, too well to subsist on a professor's salary.

His home was huge and he drove a late-model SUV with custom appointments. He also had a sleek sports car that he roared along the highway in. McKenna had seen him once when she was on her way out of town.

"All right," she conceded. She had been rude to him and that wasn't like her.

He smiled. The moment held for a second longer than necessary. Then Parker quit it when he turned back in his seat and opened his computer.

"There's one more thing," McKenna said. She couldn't believe she was about to say this, especially to a man she didn't even like. "If we're going to be together for most of the hours of the day, you can't just sit there like a silent rock."

"You want me to talk to you?" he asked, looking at her.

"Not especially. But if you're going to go with me, I don't want to be the driver and you the professor critiquing me the entire way." She shifted in her seat. "Parker, this is the trip of a lifetime. It's a chance to see a part of the world in a way we haven't seen it before. It isn't about driving. It's about the landscape, the countryside, talking to people, enjoying what God gave us." *And learning about ourselves.* The last she kept to herself.

"You're asking a lot of a restored car and an old road. Are you sure that's the real reason?"

McKenna hesitated and then decided to tell him the truth. "It's not the entire reason. It's about me, too. Who I am."

He frowned.

"I'm not going into any further explanation. It's personal, but I want to find something in myself that I've lost. Can you understand that? Don't just let the scenery go by without giving it a look."

After a minute, he nodded. She felt as if he was going to reach out and touch her. But he didn't.

For a moment she was both grateful and disappointed. It had been three years since a man had touched her. Except for bumping into Parker a few days ago and finding his arms holding her, she'd hadn't been close to a man. That small incident had reminded her that she missed it.

"Well, McKenna Wellington, it's time to start your engine."

IT DIDN'T TAKE long for the busy downtown streets of Chicago to morph into the rolling hills and open spaces of the countryside. It took longer for them to reach it, however. If McKenna had left on time, she'd have missed rush hour traffic. But her spat with Parker delayed her and she and Parker had to negotiate the bumper-to-bumper medley to get to the beginning of the journey. But they were on it now.

And her anger was almost gone. Her argument with Parker had given her a headache, but it was easing now. She'd forced herself to relax, forced her shoulders down and her breathing to return to normal. She'd even begun to play a silent game with the license tags on vehicles that passed her. It was something she used to do with her parents when they went on vacations. McKenna learned a lot of words and it was fun to stump her parents.

She smiled while remembering that as a tag went by with the letters F-T-R on it. Immediately she thought of the word *father*. After that the words came quickly and her headache was soon forgotten.

Parker hadn't said much since she started driving, but he also hadn't opened his computer and resumed his editing job. McKenna began to feel bad. She wasn't usually angry at people. It was only around Parker that her temper seemed to get the better of her.

She searched for something to say. They had little in common. He was friends with Marshall, although McKenna could never figure out why the two liked each other. Marshall was outgoing, fun loving and always up for a challenge. Parker was the stay-at-home type. He categorized everything, didn't speak much, at least not to her, and judged everyone and everything.

"Are you planning to teach in September?" McKenna finally asked.

"I am on the schedule," he said.

"Suppose we're not back by then?"

He glanced at her. "Still trying to get rid of me?"

"That's not it," she lied. She did want to get rid of him, but figured that plan was now dead. "I have no particular timetable I'm working with. I'm free as a bird and winging my way wherever the wind blows." She tossed her hair to one side, suddenly feeling the exhilaration of the journey.

"If we're still out on the road by then, I'll make the decision to either leave you high and dry or get someone to cover my classes."

He was smiling when McKenna looked at him, but she couldn't read his face. McKenna had always avoided Parker. He and Marshall often arranged to meet at a restaurant or Marshall would go to his place and pick him up when they went out. Now she couldn't tell if he was being facetious or serious.

He checked his watch. Then he pulled out his cell phone.

"Who are you calling?" she asked.

"I thought I'd check on Lydia. She should be awake by now."

McKenna reached over and took the phone from him. She turned it off and dropped it in the unused ash tray.

"Why did you do that?"

"No cell phones, except in emergencies. We're out of touch with everyone. If there's an emergency, someone else will have to deal with it."

"But I promised Lydia I'd call."

"She's going to be fine. We both heard the doctor say so. I ordered flowers to be sent to her this morning with a card that said I was leaving today. She'll know why you didn't call. And even if you did, what could you do?"

"You can't honestly expect to drive all these miles without using a phone."

"Why can't I?"

"Suppose you need something? Don't you have to check in occasionally and let people back home know you're all right?"

"No one needs to know unless there's an emergency. We can use pay phones if necessary. But I don't want to be pulled into the minutia of life back in Woodbine Heights. If something's going on there we can't fix it."

"You're a real surprise, you know that?"

"What do you mean?" McKenna asked. Her stomach clenched, ready for another of his compliments couched in a joke.

"I never would have thought anyone like you would try doing what you're doing."

"What do you mean, 'anyone like me'?"

"Don't get your back up. I mean you always appeared so grounded, so much a person who knew where everything was. When you were running the company after Marshall's death, from what Lydia told me, you were a perfect CEO, dealing with projections and next year's forecast, new products and all the duties that come with being in charge. Now you're driving off into the sunset with no set plan and only a few maps."

He looked in the small pocket in the door. McKenna had stashed the maps there.

"What is this?" She pulled a plastic container from the side of his seat.

"A DVD cover. Lydia gave me the entire set."

"Of *Route 66*?"

He nodded. "She was going to watch the old TV series, maybe duplicate Tod and Buz and their adventures in their red-and-white Corvette. She thought if I watched them it would make the trip more interesting. I loaded them on my computer."

"Tod and Buz?" McKenna raised her eyebrows.

"The characters' names in the series. Two guys, traveling the southwest and living off the land. Every episode was an adventure."

"That's right," McKenna said.

"And you're on your own adventure now?" he asked.

"I guess this means we both are."

"So which one are you, Tod or Buz?"

McKenna smiled for the first time. "Since you're the guest here, you should choose first," she said.

"Oh, no." He shook his head. "This is your fantasy. And I know nothing about Buz or Tod. You choose first."

"Tod was the sensible one. He was blond and logical, always thinking the situation through."

"Like a CEO?"

She nodded.

"So Buz was the dark angel? The one who shot first and discussed it later."

"Right!"

"I guess that makes you…"

"Buz," she answered for him.

He laughed, a hearty, belly laugh that McKenna found very pleasing. But then she remembered Marshall's laugh and it reminded her that she would never hear it again.

And part of the reason for that was Parker.

IT HAD STARTED ALREADY, McKenna acknowledged. She sat up straighter, mentally shaking herself.

Parker had begun to talk. The two of
them had had a civil conversation. McKenna
couldn't remember that ever being the case.
They'd passed each other or avoided each
other for years. Now she was sitting next to
him, close enough to feel his body heat and
smell his cologne. Who would have thought
he even wore cologne? Or that he'd speak to
her as if they were friends.

They pulled into a gas station and restaurant in Litchfield, Illinois. The Belvidere
Café, Motel and Gas Station was closed and
the building decaying, the pumps gone, but
McKenna recognized it from her research.
Only the café remained. The sign on it was
faded and worn. Awnings, sporting areas of
rust, hung over the windows.

She got out of the car and walked toward
the brown-and-tan brick one-story building. Her feet crunched on the gravel path
that had once led to a parking lot and motel
rooms. Not even a ghost of them remained.

"At this rate," Parker said. "It'll take months to get to the coast."

She looked at him. "Yes, it will," was all she said.

Pulling a camera from the back of her seat, she took photographs from every angle.

"Are you planning to write a book with all these photos?"

She snapped one of Parker. Moving the camera down so she could see his life-size image, she said, "They are only for my benefit. Memories of the trip."

Parker smiled, at least McKenna thought it was a smile. His lips pulled apart, but he said nothing, scrutinizing the building as if it had become more important thing in the world in the past three seconds.

"Give me the camera. I'll take one of you next to the building."

She did as he suggested, then went to stand below the faded sign.

"Not there," Parker directed. "Over here." He pointed to the space next to the building's single step. She moved to where he indicated. "I can get the sign and you and the building at the same time."

McKenna wondered if she should smile. She decided to do so. This was a fun trip and she felt as if they were getting somewhere, even if they were only an hour out of Chicago.

She heard the click of the shutter opening and closing.

"Don't move," he said as she began to come forward. "I'll get a few more. The building is interesting, now that I've had a chance to look at it."

Parker took several more shots before McKenna stopped him. She offered to take photos of him, but he declined.

Turning to focus on the building, McKenna thought of Marshall. This should have been his trip, their trip together. She'd considered taking it with him. The two of them had talked about it. Yet somehow the business always came first, except— McKenna stopped as Parker walked into her view. She frowned.

Parker had been with Marshall last. The ski trip. McKenna didn't like skiing. She was pretty good at ice-skating, but she felt the huge skis were unwieldy. And she hadn't wanted to be around Parker. So the two men had gone off together.

But only one had come back.

"McKenna!"

She jolted at the strength of Parker's voice.

"Are you all right?" he asked, his tone calmer.

"Fine," she said. He must have seen the look on her face. Thankfully he couldn't read her thoughts. At least she hoped he couldn't.

"You looked as if you were thinking of something painful."

"It's just the sun." She squinted at the sky. The sun was high and bright, although it wasn't the cause of her pain.

"Maybe we should get something to eat or drink," Parker suggested.

"Are you hungry already?" she asked.

"Not especially, but I would like something to drink."

McKenna had a small cooler behind her seat. It held six small bottles of water. She didn't mention it.

"Good idea," she said.

"Wow, what a car," someone said from behind Parker.

McKenna whipped around. A short man with white hair and an even whiter beard stood next to the Corvette. He was dressed in worn but clean jeans and a T-shirt bearing the faded logo of a Budweiser beer can.

"I haven't seen one of these in ages," he said. "You folks driving The 66?"

McKenna had never heard the road referred to as *The 66* before.

"We are," Parker replied.

"In this?" He indicated the car, admiration evident in his tone.

"That's our intention," McKenna stated.

His eyes came up, but his head didn't move. He reminded McKenna of a professor she once had who looked over his glasses more than through them. He was the one who told her she had no aptitude for mechanical drawing.

"Where'd you get this? Hasn't been made for years."

"Decades," McKenna corrected.

"The lady—"

"My husband and I planned it."

She and Parker had spoken at the same time. McKenna was unsure why that happened. Marshall had been on her mind and the words were out before she thought about it.

He looked at Parker. "No stuff?" he asked.

"None," Parker smiled, but did not correct the mistake.

Still, McKenna decided, she liked the man.

"In my youth, I used to work on cars. Lived back in Detroit then. Ford was my company. Never worked on one of these babies." Again the man looked at the car as if it was a past lover.

"Any idea what the road looks like ahead of us?" Parker asked. Apparently the pragmatist was rising to the surface again.

"It'll be all right for a few miles, but be careful. With a low car like this, you could pull the chassis right out from under her."

"We will," Parker said.

Both shook hands with the man and got in the car. He waited until they drove away. McKenna saw him still standing in place until the car turned the corner several blocks away. Not far from the Belvidere was the Ariston Café, also on Route 66, although the facade was reminiscent of The Alamo in San Antonio. The café had opened its doors in 1935 and was still operating.

After the photo session, which McKenna repeated, she and Parker had lunch there before getting on the road and continuing their journey. During their meal, they didn't mention the subject that was on McKenna's mind. She wondered if Parker thought of it, too.

When they were back in the Corvette, she finally brought it up.

"Back there," she began, not indicating where she meant on the road behind them or any of the places they had been since beginning this journey. "When the old man assumed you were my husband."

He glanced at her. Since McKenna was driving, she couldn't look at him for more than a second.

"Why didn't you correct him?" she asked.

For a while, Parker didn't say anything. McKenna glanced at him twice.

"He kept talking and he was so admiring the car, I didn't think anything of it. Did it bother you?"

"No," she said. It wasn't exactly the truth.

"Why did you bring it up, then?"

"Well," she hedged. "I thought it was the polite thing to do."

"Then I'd have to explain to someone not of our generation that we were traveling companions, but not lovers."

This was not going the way she assumed it would. McKenna was sorry she'd made a point of it.

"You don't think he'd understand?"

"I don't think he'd believe it."

"Why not?"

Parker didn't reply. When coaxed, he said. "Let's just say, you should look in the mirror once in a while."

McKenna was still wondering what he meant by that when the sun was going down. She knew he was married and divorced. She felt slightly uncomfortable that he hadn't spoken up to correct the old man's impression of them, but then, neither had she. And she had no reason that explained her own silence.

"Are we going to drive during the night?"

Parker interrupted her thoughts. "Or only while there's daylight?"

"During the day," she said. "I want to see what can be seen and not have to wonder about the road."

"Good idea. Glad we're on the same page with that," Parker said.

PARKER MARVELED AT the feel of the car. He understood why people stopped them on the street and in parking lots to admire the beauty of this creation. What they didn't know was what it felt like to sit behind the wheel, to drive this vehicle, to know what it meant to hug the road and corner a turn as if the car was one with the pavement. Parker felt confined with the speed limit. He wanted to open the engine up, give it its due and let it go as fast as it could.

He thought of McKenna that night on the practice track. Her face glowed under the lamp lights as she emerged from this car. Parker had never been one for most of the things men liked in life, but he loved cars. The moment he saw it sitting on the track, he knew it was something he wanted to drive.

The day was clear, and the road was theirs. If he and McKenna never agreed on anything, this car was definitely a point where they could come together. Checking on her, he saw she was watching the road. For both of them, Route 66 was a new experience. The top was down on the car and Parker felt the breeze.

THE ROAD WASN'T as bad as McKenna expected it would be, but they weren't far from Chicago yet. She'd studied maps and checked on the internet, but there was no telling if they were current. Weather from the past winter could have washed part of the blacktop away or completely broken it into shards of gravel. There was also snow-plow damage and the destructive Midwestern wind.

The speed limit was lower than the highway speed, so if there was something in their way, they would likely see it in enough time to avoid it. At least she could. She didn't know about Parker, but Marshall had told her he was a competent driver.

Maybe, she thought. She had yet to experience it. He sat silently next to her tapping keys on a small computer. The computer was a concession. He was editing a book that had a deadline. She'd agreed to him bringing it along, but not to use it to look up things about the trip. Adventure came in not knowing.

Still, she would rather talk to him than just drive. If she'd been alone, she'd play the radio, sing along to the popular songs and keep herself busy that way. With Parker, she felt as if she was being intolerant of his need to concentrate.

"What is it?" he asked.

"Excuse me?"

"There's something on your mind. I can hear it."

"Really? Then do I need to tell you what it is?"

His laugh was more a grunt. "I'm not that psychic."

"I was wondering how your book was coming."

"You were wondering if I planned to stare at my machine all the way to the Pacific Coast Highway."

McKenna smiled and relaxed her shoulders. "I guess you are psychic."

He closed the top of the machine and turned in his seat to face her. That action caused a small flutter in her stomach. She wanted to talk to him, but now that he was giving her his full attention, she was unsure of what to say.

"You're just easy to read," he said.

"I am?"

"When your mind is churning."

"I know you have a deadline for your book, so I don't want to keep you from getting it done."

"But why look at a computer screen, when there is a world out there I'm missing?" He indicated the window on her side of the car.

McKenna nodded.

"There isn't much out there. The trees and shrubs look pretty much the same as any along a highway, except these go by at a slower pace.

Wasn't that just like him? He didn't see the beauty of slowing down. McKenna contained her sigh. She may as well be alone for all the company Parker provided. For a while she thought they were going to be all right, friendly even, but he'd crawled back into the cubbyhole he'd built for himself and it wasn't large enough for anyone other than him. Not that the right woman wouldn't mind the tight squeeze.

McKenna stifled a laugh. She never thought of Parker being affectionate with a woman. He'd been divorced for years and never dated since, as far as she could remember. McKenna supposed he was set in his ways, like old people get. Lydia had said he wasn't old, but so far she saw no indication of that.

THEY HAD BARELY crossed the Illinois border into Missouri when the sun started to set. It would be dark in an hour. McKenna knew they could be farther along if she hadn't stopped to take so many pictures, but she felt no guilt over the delay. This was how she envisioned the trip, taking her time, recording what she wanted, going down paths that looked interesting.

Parker hadn't complained since asking if they were going to drive during the night.

He'd gone back to his computer screen, only offering an occasion comment on the land-scape. McKenna felt he was letting her know he could both write and watch what was happening at the same time.

When McKenna turned into the town of Carthage, he snapped the lid of his lap-top closed and looked up. McKenna could almost see the coils in his mind assessing where they were and all aspects of the area around them. She stopped the car at a gas station and looked across at Parker.

"Carthage," she said, unnecessarily.

"Missouri?" Parker asked.

McKenna confirmed.

"If we stop now, we could get something to eat and find a place to stay for the night?" Parker suggested. "There'll be enough light for us to walk around the town and see some of it."

"Good idea," McKenna said.

They both got out of the car and Parker had the pump in his hands when two guys approached them.

"Man, what I would give for one of these," one of them said, obviously in awe. He was wearing a nondescript colored uniform that looked as if it was a combination of dark green and jet-black oil. Over the pocket the name Nick had been stitched into the fabric.

Parker turned to her and raised his eyebrows as if they had a secret. McKenna nodded with a smile. Parker returned it and for a long moment she held it.

"Where did you find such a treasure?" the man without Nick on his uniform asked. McKenna's attention was pulled away from her traveling companion.

She watched the two men admiring the car. The second man was wearing the same color uniform as the first, only the name on his pocket said Willie. Willie moved around the car, perusing it as if it were a spaceship that might take off at any second, yet the fascination was too much to ignore.

"I didn't find it," Parker said. "The lady built it." He turned to include McKenna as she came level with them.

"Is that the honest truth?" Both of them stared at her, clearly assessing whether to believe Parker or not. Then their eyes went back to the Corvette.

"She's quite ingenious," Parker said, still gesturing at McKenna. His gaze made her warm and she scanned the ground until Parker pulled the gas hose out of the car and replaced the cap.

"What kind of engine does it have?" Nick asked.

McKenna wasn't sure if this was a test or not, but she decided to let them know she knew her stuff. Since both men had come through the door of the station and not one of the open bays, and they were both dressed alike, she was unsure if one or both were mechanics.

"It's a 283-cubic-inch engine. It has the power of 230 horses. The original Wonderbar AM/FM radio is installed along with a cassette player. The car is a soft top with the original Roman Red paint and white coves, T-10 transmission, 3.55 rear, stainless exhaust, sun visors, windshield washers, courtesy light, heater, seat belts, hubcaps and wide white radials. And she drives like a dream."

"Da-mn," Nick said, stretching the word into two syllables. His voice was full of awe.

McKenna knew he was imagining himself behind the wheel, speeding through the countryside, his foot to the floor as the mighty engine released its power on the straightaway. She recognized those feelings. They'd coursed through her own veins the first time she took it out and couldn't resist not having it tap its full potential.

"Is there a place around here we can get something to eat, maybe find a motel to stay the night?" Parker asked.

They got directions, paid for the gas and set out, leaving two awestruck attendants in their wake.

"We can probably expect this kind of reception anytime we park this car," Parker said. He was relaxed, his arm across the back of her seat. It wasn't touching her, but it might as well have been. McKenna could feel the hairs on the back of her neck stand at attention. And the heat from his fingers tinged the air between them and caressed her neck. With her hair secured in a ponytail, she could feel the redness spread around her nape.

"I know," she replied. "It's one of the reasons I chose to build it."

"What do you mean by that?"

"A trip of this length means you need to meet people. The car is a way of doing that."

"You have everything planned out, down to the last detail. Are you sure you want to be Buz? You're acting more like Tod."

"That was before we left. Now that all the planning is done, the execution is whatever comes."

She pulled into a parking space on the main street in front of a café with gingham curtains covering the lower part of the window. Before they were out of the car, people had begun to peer between the curtains at them. Parker exited the car and came around to open her door. McKenna was surprised. He offered his hand and helped her up from the low riding vehicle. Once she was standing, he dropped his hand.

Inside, McKenna chose a table near the windows. Every eye in the place followed their movement.

"That's a great car," a man of about thirty at the next table said before the waitress came over. "I don't believe I've ever seen one of those."

"'59 Corvette." McKenna answered his unasked question.

"'59, huh?" Another man left his table and the woman with him to come over and stare out through the window. McKenna estimated his age at around sixty. He wore a short haircut and jeans and shirt that seemed as if they'd seen many days of hard work. "What a beauty. And she looks like she just came off the assembly line."

A small gathering of people had left the restaurant to get a better look at the car.

"Almost," McKenna stated, not explaining anything further.

"Is she yours?" He swung his gaze between the two of them.

McKenna nodded.

"Wanna sell her?"

McKenna's eyes opened wide. It was the last question she'd expected. The idea of selling the car had never entered her mind. It had a purpose and while she'd put it together it had become part of her personality. Selling it wasn't an option.

"It's not for sale," she said.

"Well, if you change your mind, give me a call." He took a business card from his shirt pocket and thrust it toward Parker.

"It's the lady's car," Parker said. "She's done everything for it except date it."

McKenna gave him a startled look.

"How'd you happen to come by a car like this?" the thirtysomething asked.

"Always wanted a Corvette. I have a couple of brothers who were interested in cars," she answered.

"One of them restore this for you?"

"Afraid not," McKenna told him. "Restored it myself."

"You're a woman after my own heart," the sixty-year-old said. The woman he'd left behind at his table made a rude noise.

"I love you, honey," he tossed over his shoulder. "But this is a *car*." He looked at McKenna with a quiet appreciation in his eyes. "When I was a boy, a guy down the street from me had one of these. We always knew when he was coming or going." He shook his head, as if remembering a better time in his life. "Man, did the girls go for him."

"If you'll all move away, I'll take their order," the waitress said.

McKenna and Parker acknowledged the woman, dressed in a skirt and a tight T-shirt, and gave their order. While the café patrons moved back to their tables, the discussion remained on the car, with everyone participating as if they were all from the same family, discussing an amusing incident that had just occurred.

"What's your name?" a woman asked.

"McKenna Wellington," she said. "This is Parker Fordum."

"Y'all married?"

"No," Parker replied. "We're driving buddies. This is Buz and I'm Tod."

"Yeah?" an old woman spoke from a dark corner. She got up and walked over to them. Pointing a finger, she punctuated the air in a staccato cadence as if she were tapping out a message. "Buz and Tod. And that car. Don't sound real to me. I remember that television program. What was it?" Her question

was directed inward. She was trying to remember.

"Route 66," Parker answered.

"Are you one of them?" the sixty-year old
asked.

"One of them?" McKenna frowned.

"Every year people come through here,
driving Route 66. Some even claim they're
going to make it all to way to Santa Monica."

"That's our goal," McKenna confirmed.

"Good luck," he snorted.

"What does that mean?" McKenna's back
went up.

The man's companion, at least his age
joined them. He ignored her and glanced
through the window again. "It's a nice-
looking car, but impractical for a trip like
that. You'll tear it up trying to stay on that
road." He scratched his head. "Now, if you
sell it to me, I'll do right by it."

He gave McKenna and Parker the once-
over. Both were frowning.

"The road is rough. The car is low to the
ground. It doesn't have front-wheel drive,
much less the four-wheel drive you'll need

in many of the places where the road just fades into a field or the blacktop has totally disappeared. If it rains and the ground is muddy, you could be stuck in a place with no traffic or help."

"You paint a rather sullen picture," Parker pointed out. "Have you driven the route?"

"Took my daughter five years ago. We got as far as Oklahoma before giving up and getting on the highway."

"We intend to make it all the way, low carriage or not," Parker said.

McKenna felt a bubble of pride well up inside her. Parker hadn't joined the ranks of the disbelievers, but supported her and her quest. She glanced at him, mentally thanking him for watching her back.

She guessed he was thawing. He didn't appear as stiff as he had when they'd started this trip. And they'd only been gone a day. Maybe by the end of the trip, she'd understand why Marshall was his friend and why Lydia insisted he was different from the person McKenna thought he was. Thinking of Marshall brought to mind other memories of him and Parker. Maybe there was something else she could find out.

The waitress brought their food, interrupting McKenna's speculation. Her stomach growled, letting her know how hungry she was. She'd ordered a chef's salad and bottled water. One of her goals was to eat healthy and get exercise along the way, so she wouldn't be tired and resort to terminating the trip. She and Parker were alternating driving every two hours.

She remembered when he first got behind the wheel earlier today. They'd stopped at a gas station. Returning from the ladies' room, she saw Parker eyeing the car as if it was candy. It was like sex at sixteen. All the boyhood fantasies came to life in the way he scanned the red interior. Like the two guys at the service station, he circled the car as if it were a living, breathing thing. It seemed to epitomize what he viewed as the ultimate beauty. Something so striking and so unattainable that he'd never thought he'd see it in his lifetime. Yet here it was, waiting for him to slide behind the wheel and turn the key. She'd told him to drive it alone for a few miles, then come back and get her.

"I guess you'll be staying here the night and leaving in the morning," the sixty-year-old said from across the room. He'd returned to his table and so had the older woman he was with. "It's best to do the driving during the day."

"I agree," McKenna said.

"You'll like the hotel. Not many people there now. Give us a couple of weeks and the place will be overrun with travelers heading somewhere. Most stop because of the sign."

"Sign?" Parker asked.

"Yeah, didn't you see it? It's a big billboard leading people here."

Neither of them had seen a sign saying anything like that, but Parker nodded as if he had.

"Mind if I go out and take a look at the car?" The thirtysomething stepped in front of the table and asked his question. It was a moot point, since there were already people outside, but he showed he had manners.

"Be my guest," McKenna said.

As the rest of the admirers filed out, the

waitress shooed the others away from her and Parker. "Give them some room," she said. "They came here to eat. The rest of you go back to your own meals."

Only people who knew each other well could talk to each other like that. And only in a small town. Her words were taken to heart and the onlookers returned to their places. A couple of them joined the gathering on the sidewalk at the car. McKenna and Parker dug in to their meals.

"Can I ask you a question?" Parker said after a few minutes of silence.

McKenna's heart pumped a little faster. "Sure," she answered.

"Are you afraid?"

"Afraid of what?"

"Of this trip? Of going into the unknown?"

"I'm not leaving the planet," she laughed, buying herself some time.

Parker sat back in his seat. "I know you get upset when I mention you're a woman, but barring that point, you were willing to go off on this trip alone. You have no idea who you'd meet along the way. And in that car…" He glanced toward the window. "You could be putting yourself in real danger."

"There's always the highway. It's my backup plan, but I don't expect to use it."

"You could get stuck somewhere and the highway may be too far to reach, like the older gentleman mentioned. If anyone comes along, they may have another agenda."

McKenna shuddered at the coldness of his words, but she wouldn't let him know. "Parker, if I concede that I am a woman, vulnerable and weak compared to a man, would you let this be the last time you mention my gender in relationship to safety?"

He stared at her for a long time. Then he nodded.

McKenna sipped her drink and set it on the table. For a moment she thought about what she wanted to say. "I do have some anxiety about the *unknown*," she said. "I suppose it's natural to be afraid of what you don't know. But it's also exciting. I'm going over ground that's known as America's highway. This is how our parents traveled. In cars, without credit cards, iPods or global positioning systems."

"Wait a minute. What do you mean no credit cards?"

"No credit cards. We're doing this strictly with cash."

"What if we run out? And with no set dates, there's no way to gauge our spending. It's inevitable that we'll run out of money somewhere."

"Spoken like a true economist," McKenna said, unable to resist the barb.

"What is the big deal with using credit cards?" he scoffed. "From the videos I've watched and what Lydia told me, those guys you're emulating had plenty of money."

"Cash. They had plenty of cash. When they didn't have any, they got jobs and worked until they had enough to get to the next town," McKenna explained.

"That's only because they were too stupid to carry plastic."

"That's because they were free and had no real address. They were rich enough to have lawyers and accountants to take care of things at home while they went out and discovered the world."

"You do realize that was a television program and not real life?" Parker said.

McKenna scowled at him. "We'll only use the cards if there is absolutely no other choice. Or we need medical services."

"You're making this trip intentionally hard."

"You didn't have to come."

"Let's not go there." He paused. "We've been doing fine being civil to each other."

She dropped her shoulders. "All right, I apologize for my remark. But we're not using credit cards. I have ample cash. And if we do run out, we'll find jobs and do what Buz and Tod did."

"You *are* crazy," he said.

"I've been accused of worse."

CHAPTER FOUR

PARKER DIDN'T KNOW whether to kick himself or to explode with laughter. He'd long admired McKenna Wellington, although her opinion of him was rather cool. She was brave and competent. He knew this in the way she'd taken charge after her husband died and kept their business operating. For the families working for them, it kept food on their tables and a roof over their heads. But he didn't know about this wild streak in her.

When Lydia told him her scheme to drive Route 66 all the way to the beach, he'd thought it was a passing notion. That a woman with her responsibilities and her earnest nature would eventually see the impracticality of such an action. But he'd learned that once an idea got into McKenna's head, she flew with it and only changed it when she knew there was absolutely no way it would work. So far she hadn't learned that about this expedition. At least not yet.

He'd been appalled when he learned that Lydia was going to go with her. He had reservations about the two of them traveling alone across the country. Life wasn't as safe now as it had been when Route 66 was a popular television show. But Lydia proved as stalwart as McKenna in her determination to accompany her friend.

Parker didn't know whether Lydia's broken leg was a good thing or a bad thing. It had kept her home and opened the door for him to at least do what he could to keep McKenna out of trouble. So far everything had gone smoothly. After the scene in her garage, they'd spoken to each other without arguing too much.

The road, too, hadn't been that bad. Speed limits were lower than they were on the major highways so their miles covered were less than normal, but that was to be expected. He also had to admit that he liked watching the scenery. He hadn't been on a car trip since he was a child with his parents, usually en route to camp or to visit his grandparents. His trips as an adult had been on airplanes or trains. And often he'd had his head buried in a book. He wasn't sure how he'd feel when they got to mile 2,400, but he'd take it one mile at a time for now.

McKenna was an enigma. Most of what he knew about her came from his friendship with Lydia and the few parties where they'd both been guests. He and Marshall were friends, and while Marshall talked about her, it was her work he usually focused on. So far Parker knew she was headstrong and had a plan, even if she did think she was Buz. However, there remained 2,000 miles in front of them. He'd certainly have the chance to get to know her better. And maybe change her mind about a few things.

The motel they found to spend the night in must have been built before there was a national highway system. The place was a small collection of cramped cabins. The beds were twin-size and the sink hung from a wall in the corner. Above it was a dark mirror that barely reflected an image. Parker already knew he was longer than the bed. Sleeping wasn't going to be comfortable.

McKenna was in the cabin next to his. Quickly he checked the window, noting the view as if he was in a high-rise luxury hotel overlooking Lake Michigan. What he saw was the next cabin thirty feet away, weathered and sporting walls of chipped paint. He wondered if the locks still worked on the doors and made a mental note to check McKenna's.

The knock on his door reminded him that he and McKenna were going to go for a walk. He let her in. She'd changed clothes and appeared as fresh as she had that morning when they left Chicago.

"Ready?" she asked.

Nodding, they headed out. The motel was on Route 66 and they strolled back toward the town. It didn't take long for them to reach the main street. It was a quiet town outside of Carthage. He noticed the name on the sign said Wheaton. They crossed a bridge over the Wheaton River and walked up a tree-lined street.

"Pretty," McKenna said. It was the first

thing she'd spoken since they'd begun walking. The silence was companionable. Parker thought it best to let her take the lead. This was her adventure. She lifted her camera and took a picture.

Again, they lapsed into silence. Parker searched his mind for something to say, but could think of nothing. As they passed a library made of red brick, he asked, "Is this what we're going to do in every town? Find a place to stay, eat, take a walk and a few pictures?"

"We're going to do what feels right, feels natural."

"This feels natural?"

She nodded and smiled.

"You are a strange one," Parker said.

"Strange, how?"

"I suppose I never thought you'd do something like this. Where does this wanderlust come from?"

"You really want to know?"

"Yes. I do."

"When I graduated from high school, I wanted to study languages. I wanted to travel the world, learn all about other people and other cultures. I wanted to talk to people and find out how they lived. I wanted to hike in the mountains and spend time in a small town. Instead, I studied business, married Marshall, learned about batteries, automobiles, robotics, acid corrosion, and never went farther than New York City to an auto convention. So, after Marshall died, I stepped up to save the company. But I thought about how short life is and if I was ever going to do the things I wanted to do, I had to do them now." She glanced at him. "How about you? Was economics what you wanted to do from the beginning?"

He took a moment to answer, remembering the dreams of his youth. "I always wanted to teach. At first I was going to teach grade school, but when UC offered me a job, I took it. Been there ever since."

"Nothing more? You didn't want to race cars or fly airplanes, sail out into the lake and swim to shore?"

He laughed. "Or drive 2,400 miles to the beach?"

"Something like that."

"I did." He sobered. "I wanted to write

music. Maybe play in a band. Instead I write textbooks."

McKenna stopped and turned toward him. "That's wonderful. Why didn't you?"

"It wasn't practical."

"Who told you that? Your father?"

His eyes widened at her perception. "He said playing in a band was fine for weekends, but I needed a profession to fall back on. So I studied accounting and finance. I liked economics and took more courses in it. In graduate school I tutored other students. And finally I got the offer. It was practical to accept it."

"Parker, you need to do the impractical. Life is too short to walk the straight line." The last sentence was delivered quietly but with a passion so strong it reached out and touched him.

They didn't discuss it any further, but mutually agreed to return to the motel and get a good night's sleep. Parker thought about what she'd told him and what he'd told her. He'd nearly forgotten his dream of being in a band. Of course, he had a music collection to rival the best, and he enjoyed picking out a tune on the piano, but he'd lost that drive to write music. He spent all his time correcting papers and preparing the next edition of his textbook or some paper that needed publishing. He hadn't tried his hand at a song in years.

And now, with McKenna, being part of her dream made him regret the death of his own.

McKenna stopped abruptly just before they reached her cabin. Parker looked at her. Her face was frozen in horror, her mouth open.

"What?" Parker said.

She pointed rather than spoke. Then she took off in a fast run. A second later, Parker followed.

"McKenna, no," he shouted.

The door to her cabin stood wide open and she was about to enter. Horrible thoughts went through his mind. Someone had been in her room. They could still be there. She could walk in on a robbery in progress. They could have guns or knives. Parker stepped up his pace, but she was already through the door.

He rushed in behind her, knowing it was the wrong thing to do. She'd stopped short. He plowed into her back, his arms going around her waist and picking her up off the floor. Pulling her out of her room, he pinned her against the wooden wall with his body. He both felt and heard her breathing. It was hot against his neck. She resisted, but Parker held her tight.

"Someone could still be in there," he whispered. "Let me go first."

Parker released her and looked around. The room was empty and in a shambles. Someone had thrown her clothes all over the place.

"Stay here," he ordered, extending a hand behind him. He was ready to push her back if she tried to move.

Going to the bathroom, he found the small space trashed, but empty. Approaching the closet door, he found it, too, had only clothes strewn on the floor. Nodding to McKenna, she pushed away from the doorjamb and rushed to her locked bag she'd evidently put in the bottom dresser drawer. It was now lying open on the floor. The locks were broken. She sank to her knees, rifling through the inside, searching but not finding what she sought. Her shoulders dropped in defeat.

"It's all gone," she said. Her voice flat, resigned and unemotional. "My cash, traveler's checks, everything."

Parker assumed she would have broken down and cried, but her eyes were dry. There was nothing she could do to remedy the situation.

"I'll call the police," he said. He picked up the phone and let the office know that they needed the police.

"What about your cabin?" McKenna asked when he hung up. "Is everything all right there?"

He hadn't thought of his own belongings. "I'll be right back."

Parker went to his cabin. McKenna followed him. It was a mirror of hers, clothes strewn over the floor as if someone had been searching for something.

"What about your computer?"

"It's in the car."

They both turned and ran to the Corvette. It was fine. Nothing was out of place. The computer was in the concealed area behind the seats. Parker lifted it out.

"I don't think we should leave anything in the car from now on."

McKenna reached in and removed the DVDs and portable player that Lydia had planned to use before her accident. They went back to McKenna's cabin. Automatically, she began packing her things back in the suitcase.

"Don't do that," Parker said. "Wait for the police."

She stopped.

"What's missing?" Parker asked gently.

She turned to him. "Other than the money, a few pieces of jewelry. Nothing sentimental. I left all that at home. I have some cash in my purse. That's all that's left."

Parker nodded. "At least we can get the money back for the traveler's checks."

McKenna turned her back on him, whipping around as if she were a spinning top. "What's wrong?" Parker asked.

"My book is gone."

"Someone stole your book?"

She nodded.

"Why?"

"I don't know."

"You can get another book," Parker told her.

"The receipt for the traveler's checks was in it," she said flatly.

Parker wanted to go to her and tell her everything would be all right. He wanted to take her in his arms, but he stayed where he was for a long moment. Then his feet carried him across the space and he pulled her against him. Dry-eyed, she leaned into his shoulder, her arms circling his waist. Together they stayed that way for a few seconds. When they heard the police arriving, they separated.

The cops took a report. There was little more they could do than that. The robbers had stolen the cash. Both of them had their credit cards with them. McKenna had very few clothes and although they were scattered about the floor, nothing except the money was missing. She told the two police officers who arrived that she'd brought a few pieces of jewelry, earrings and a necklace, but they'd been in the car and were safe.

Parker related a similar story. Nothing had been taken from his room.

Soon the police were gone, leaving behind their apologies and telling them it was unlikely that the culprit would be found or the money returned. Once the officers had pulled the door shut, McKenna went back to packing. Her hands moved methodically, but Parker could tell she was shaken.

"Let me help you," Parker said.

McKenna did not change her position. He crouched to the floor and helped her retrieve her strewn garments. When everything was in the canvas bag she used for the few clothes and toiletries she'd brought, she got up from the floor and walked to the small dresser containing a mirror that looked as old as the Mother Road itself.

"Parker?"

Again he wanted to go to her, enfold her in his arms and tell her everything would be all right, but he stood where he was and said nothing.

"I can't stay here alone. Would you mind if I stayed in your room?"

He moved then. He went over and closed

her small bag, then lifted it from the floor. "Do you have everything?"

She scanned the small room. The space was orderly again, except for the bed. The sheets and blanket had been ripped from the mattress, which lay askew over the box spring.

She nodded and they went out the door. A small crowd had gathered when the police cars had arrived. The motel manager and his wife were also there.

"Ms. Wellington, my wife and I apologize. I assure you nothing like this has ever happened before."

McKenna nodded and Parker put his arm around her waist and guided her away from the prying eyes.

"We'll move you to different cabins," the manager's wife offered.

"That won't be necessary," McKenna assured her. "We'll be fine. Thank you." She offered her a weak smile and Parker applied pressure to her back.

"Are you sure?" the woman asked again.

McKenna nodded.

"Then I'll have a maid come over and restore the rooms."

"We'll be all right," Parker said. "No need to arouse anyone else."

"At least, we can change the lock," the manager said. Together he and his wife moved toward the motel office.

McKenna headed for Parker's cabin.

"Do you think they'll come back?" she asked when he closed the door on the curious onlookers.

"No," he said decisively. He really didn't know, but she was already worried enough. He didn't want to upset her any more than she was already.

McKenna studied the two beds. She chose the one he had not decided to sleep in and began restoring it to order.

"Let me help you?" He moved toward her, but she turned and stopped him, her hands on his arms. He felt the slight tremor in her fingers.

"Parker, I'm all right." She dropped her hands. "I admit I'm a little upset, but it will pass."

He stepped back, going to make up his

own bed and restoring his belongings to order.

A soft knock on the door produced the locksmith. He introduced himself and made quick work of changing the lock and checking its security.

"I'll change the other one," he said. Extending his hand toward McKenna with two keycards in it, he said, "These will work, ma'am."

McKenna took the electronic keys.

"I'm real sorry about the break in," he said.

She nodded, but said nothing. Her face was pale and her eyes looked large. Parker recognized shock.

"Your keys, sir." He passed a separate set of keycards to Parker and left them alone. Parker went to the bathroom and filled two plastic cups with water.

"Drink this," he told McKenna.

She looked up at him.

"It's water," he told her. "I wish it was vodka, but it's only water."

Taking the first cup, she drank it all. He passed her the second one and she drained it. When she handed the cup back to him, he checked her temperature with the back of his hand. It felt normal. Her skin wasn't cold or clammy.

"Do you feel dizzy?"

She shook her head.

"Weak?"

Again she shook her head.

He breathed a little easier. His body relaxed, although he was unaware of the tension within himself.

"I didn't realize you'd had medical training," McKenna said.

"I haven't, but I've handled an emergency or two."

McKenna frowned, but eventually her face relaxed. For twenty minutes she was quiet, then went to the sink and brushed her teeth. From there she moved into the tiny bathroom, which held a toilet and shower stall. There was hardly room enough to turn around. He heard the shower squeal and wondered if it was masking tears which she was surely entitled to.

Later, when the door opened, a rush of hot fragrant steam came out. McKenna stood there. She'd pulled her hair back into a pony-tail. It was partially wet from her shower. She wore a long T-shirt that stopped at her knees.

Parker had his computer on his lap and was trying to concentrate on his edits. Her appearance ended that.

"I'm done," she said. She moved to the bed next to his and sat down on it. "I'm sorry this happened. Lydia and I planned to share sleeping quarters. I'm sorry to intrude on you."

"McKenna." Parker closed the computer, knowing he wasn't going to do any more work tonight. "If you hadn't asked to come here, I would have asked to stay in your cabin. You're not an intrusion. Just try to get the robbery out of your head and sleep."

He went into the bathroom and took his own shower. Only the water he turned on was much cooler than the hot fragrance that had accompanied her.

IT FELT STRANGE to have a man in the room with her who wasn't Marshall. Parker's sounds were different. Marshall's became white noise after a while. And she hadn't thought of the way he moved around, rolled over, grunted in his sleep, in a year. But now she reluctantly had a comparison.

She listened to the rhythm of Parker's breathing. It didn't reflect that of her husband. The sound was soft and systematic. Unlike Marshall, Parker didn't snore. She rather liked all the noise. More the solidarity of knowing he was there. Tears filled McKenna's eyes, but she brushed them aside. She missed Marshall, missed him holding her in the night, missed his laugh and the wonderful way he used to surprise her with love notes he'd slip inside a desk drawer or even a box of tools he was sure she would open.

She hadn't thought about his sounds or his wistful antics in a long while. When he first died and she slept alone, she missed cuddling up to his warmth in the bed. But now she realized there was so much more that had gone with his death.

Turning over, she faced away from Parker's side of the room. She closed her eyes, wondering if sleep would come in this new environment. She doubted it would.

"McKenna?"

She thought Parker was asleep.

"Are you all right?" he asked.

She flipped onto her back and looked over in his direction. He was propped up on an elbow, staring at her.

"I knew you weren't asleep."

She wondered how that was the case. She was quiet, breathing evenly. As was he. "I was thinking," she said, buying herself a moment to answer his question.

"About what?"

"Our trip," she lied.

"What about it?"

McKenna pushed herself up and squinted across the darkness. "I was thinking we might want to do some of those things that you mentioned you wished you'd done."

He laughed.

"I'm serious."

"I doubt we have time for me to pull out my saxophone and brush up on today's music so that I can either join or form a rock band."

She heard both the sarcasm and joking in his voice. McKenna was surprised she could distinguish between the two when it came to Parker. Maybe it was due to their proximity over the past few days. Like any observant person, she'd picked up on the many habits and methods of non-verbal communication that folks unknowingly share. Parker kept most of his reserved, yet McKenna was discovering them one by one.

"I'm sure we could find a comedy club or a place where they'd let you play your instrument." He started to say something, but she anticipated it and cut him off. "And we can rent an instrument."

"Are you forgetting we're tight on money?" he asked.

"Don't be so practical. For once in your life, let go." Her voice was stronger than she'd expected. In a more normal tone, she said. "We'll find a couple of jobs and work to pay the rental fee. And any other expenses we'll have."

"Go to sleep, McKenna."

THE MORNING SUNLIGHT was warm and bright. Parker could almost forget the trauma of the night before if it wasn't for the silence in the room. McKenna moved about gathering her belongings, packing her toiletries, while not a word passed her lips.

She'd pretended to be asleep when he returned from his shower, but he knew she was awake. He'd broached the subject of them returning to Chicago. She'd shut him down faster than she'd spun the Corvette around that track the night she tested its performance.

This morning her silence spoke for her.

Parker took their bags and loaded them in the car. McKenna came out and headed for the driver's side.

"McKenna, you're being unreasonable." Parker faced her across the expanse of the Corvette. With her hands leaning on the low hood and the width of the car only a smidgen over six feet, he could reach across and touch her, shake some sense into her.

"Get this through your head, I am not going back." She spoke each word distinctly. "If you want to return to Chicago, that's your right. I'm perfectly willing to drop you at the nearest bus or train station. If you wish, I can drive you to the airport or even a rental car company. Your choice. But I am going to California." She took a deep breath.

Parker walked to her side of the car and took her arm. "Be reasonable, McKenna. We're not that far from home. Going back is the logical thing to do."

McKenna jerked away from him. "Don't tell me to be reasonable. Why do you think I'm being unreasonable? This is what I want to do. And I am going to do it."

"When did you become so obstinate?" Parker asked.

"I believe you once told me it was one of my best qualities."

She glared at him. After a moment, Parker shook his head. He was defeated. McKenna wasn't going to be turned around on this question. He knew part of her argument was bravado. The theft had rattled her. He could tell by the ashen nature of her face last night and it hadn't completely disappeared this morning.

"I'm not ending my trip over some small setback."

"Small setback! You've lost all your money. I have credit cards, which you refuse to use. If we'd come back any earlier, we might have been killed."

He deliberately watched her for a reaction. Fear flickered in her eyes, but she quickly doused it.

"We have one other recourse," he said.

"What?"

"There's an ATM in the lobby."

"They didn't have ATMs in the '60s."

"We're not in the 1960s. And even if they didn't have ATMs, they had banks. We have accounts. We can go and get more money."

McKenna waved off the idea. "Buz, we don't have a bank account. We only have *cash*."

"And little of that," he replied.

"We can't."

"Why?" Parker spread his hands, looking at her as if she'd lost her mind. No doubt Buz and Tod heard it on the radio in the Corvette.

"They had no bank account."

She couldn't be serious. "McKenna, that is a fantasy. Open your eyes."

McKenna moved a step closer to Parker. With a low menacing voice, she said. "We will not have this argument all the way to

California. We take what happens. We deal with it. Only in dire emergencies do we revert to the way things are now."

"So what happens next? What recourse do we have?"

"I have six hundred dollars. We can make do with that for a while," McKenna replied.

"Six hundred is nothing. It's going to cost us a couple thousand just for gas. Then there's lodging, tolls, food and emergencies. Even if we live like paupers, we won't make it on that."

"Well, when it's gone, we'll get jobs and work until we have enough to go on. That was the deal, Parker. Take it or leave it."

He glared at her, but she wouldn't back down. Her hair was still in last night's ponytail, although it was freshly brushed and redone. She wore little makeup, yet her face glowed with an aliveness he'd rarely seen in a woman. The vulnerability that had shaken her last night, forcing her to toss and turn in bed, crawling from one position to another for an hour, had been eradicated with the morning sun.

She was determined. They would go on

or *she* would go without him. He couldn't allow that.

"All right," he conceded. "But I'll drive the first leg."

She handed over the keys without argument. After a short stop at the office to return the cabin keys and receive another apology and a return of their lodging payment, compliments of the motel, they were off again.

After a few miles, Parker had to bring up the subject of finances. He was an economist by profession, but a pragmatist by necessity.

"In order to make this money last as long as possible, we have to make some decisions."

"I know," McKenna said. "Please don't take this the wrong way, Parker, but sleeping in the same room last night proved to me that we can cut our living expenses in half if we share a room. Is that going to be fine with you? You can say no, and I won't take it as an insult."

He swallowed, keeping his eyes on the road while his hands gripped the steering wheel. He'd been aware of her presence. The way she stood in the open doorway with her nightshirt on. The trail of scent she'd left when she came out of the bathroom. And the way she'd lain in the bed next to his. Sleeping next to her night after night was going to be a test, but she was right in her logic. With their funds being so low, and lodging being a huge amount of their daily expenditure, only having one room versus two was a vast savings.

"I sometimes snore in my sleep," Parker warned.

"If I could live with Marshall's snoring, I can do with yours," she said. "So we agree on that, sharing a room, I mean."

"I estimate that six hundred dollars can get us as far as Oklahoma. With the five hundred I have we could make it to Arizona or New Mexico, depending on gas prices. But that will only cover the gas."

"It leaves us nothing in the way of incidentals. Things we might find in a village or town that we'd love to have and can ship home."

"Not to mention sleeping in places clear of spiders and other crawling creatures,"

Parker commented, as he nodded at her in agreement.

"I guess you're right. That's not how I want to travel. We might need to get hired somewhere just to make sure we're not worried about every dime," McKenna told him. "And eating is…obviously a necessity."

The way she said it made him think she was looking forward to the adventure as if it was a sixty-minute television episode in which everything is neatly tied up by the last commercial.

"What can you do?" he asked.

McKenna stared at him, her eyes as hard as rocks.

"I mean besides being president of an auto parts company and Corvette restorer. I doubt you'll find a vacancy in either job area."

"I doubt there'll be a call for an economics professor to stand in for a few days, either." She matched his sarcasm.

He laughed and after a long moment her mouth turned into a smile and then she laughed, too. It seemed they battled over almost everything. But he admired her stamina. She stood up to his arguments and he knew nothing was going to keep her from this trip. From now on he wanted to make sure the experience was a happy one, even if they only had eleven hundred dollars between them and several unavailable and for-emergency-use-only credit cards. But they had a lot of guts and a sense of adventure. Don Quixote and Sancho couldn't have been better equipped.

THEY COULD DRIVE until the money ran out, McKenna thought when they were once again on the road. She knew neither of them would choose that option. Glancing at Parker, who was driving, she saw he stared at the road ahead. She considered what he must be thinking of her. For a while last night she believed she'd chipped that square that he boxed everyone, including himself, in. But their recent discussion had shown she was wrong.

He drove easily and with confidence. Keeping to the lower speed limit meant they were using less gas than if they were on the highway, but it also meant more slowing down and speeding up was necessary. If the

Corvette was a hybrid of today, that kind of driving would be advantageous, but this car had a 283-HP engine and she could feel that Parker wanted to open it up the way she had on the race track.

McKenna felt she should apologize, but she wasn't going to. She was only sorry about the strength of her voice, not her words. They would cope, adapt, survive. She had to know if she could do this. Why, she wouldn't even tell herself, but it was important. She'd had an easy life after the business took off. They had a fine home, with a staff to take care of the details, vacations in the best places and all the luxuries money could buy, but there was something missing in her life. McKenna felt it was the struggle, the need to accomplish something just for herself.

She'd told no one about her trip except her four close friends. She didn't want the press to know, didn't want her vice presidents to know. She wanted to complete this adventure as an anonymous citizen, not as a publicity stunt to garner more sales for the business.

Again she glanced at Parker. His attention was still on the road, although at forty-five miles an hour he could look away for an instant. She wondered if he thought she was making this journey for some other reason. She'd told him it was something she and Marshall were planning to do, but that wasn't the whole of it. It was more her idea than Marshall's. After he died, the idea returned to her and took root. Now something she couldn't define drove her to find whatever had been missing. Maybe that something was inside of her, but she had to find it.

"What are you thinking?" Parker asked, breaking into her thoughts. "You're not still angry that I told you returning was better than going on, are you?"

"I wasn't thinking about that at all," she skirted his question.

"Then from the expression on your face, it must have had something to do with Marshall."

McKenna couldn't believe how fast her head whipped around to face him. How could he know? No one knew her well enough to read her expressions, not even Marshall.

"I was thinking about Marshall," she admitted, regretting the words the moment they fell from her lips. Her husband was a subject she and Parker should not and would not discuss.

"Do you still think of him every day?"

McKenna noticed his voice was guarded. She waited a long time, deciding what to say, or if she would say anything. Finally, she spoke. "I moved his photo from my bedside table."

That was it, all she would say. If they went any further, they'd get to Marshall's death and McKenna wasn't sure she could keep her emotions under control if they did. She couldn't help thinking of Marshall. He had been an important part of her life. It was normal, she thought.

"That's good," Parker said.

McKenna stared through the windshield. "What time do you think we'll get to the next town?" She changed the subject.

"I'm not sure. Are you tired?"

She shook her head. The scenery hadn't changed much in the past hour.

"I suppose we should begin looking for

a place," he said. Parker glanced at her. McKenna could tell he was unsure if the remnants of last night's encounter were still present in her mind. They were, but she pushed them as far away as she could.

"I'm sorry," McKenna said.

"Sorry for what?"

"For yesterday. For last night."

"It wasn't your fault," Parker told her. "You couldn't know someone would break in. Be thankful we weren't there and that we still have the car."

"I am, but…" she stopped.

"But what?" he prompted.

It took a while for her to speak. Parker's compassion warred with her opinion of him. She expected him to be pragmatic, not tuned into how violated she felt.

"How I spoke to you. I shouldn't have been so…harsh."

"I can take it," he said.

McKenna knew he was shrugging off his true feelings.

"I'm starting to think you can."

She was smiling when he glanced at her again. He smiled back.

"I've never done anything like this, never even thought of it. But it might be fun," Parker conceded. "Adventurous for sure."

Her smile widened as she looked at him. For some reason that she couldn't explain, her heart did a tiny flip and Parker gripped the steering wheel harder.

CHAPTER FIVE

"SINCE YOU'VE STUDIED this road, what do you think our chances are in this car?"

Parker was driving. McKenna sat in the passenger seat. She felt weird in that spot. She hadn't ever spent this much time in it before. She loved to drive and even while Marshall was alive, she was the main driver whenever the two of them went out together.

Parker was competent. He drove the manual transmission like a pro. There was no initial start and stop before getting started whenever he was behind the wheel. He got in, adjusted the seat position and the mirrors and turned over the ignition as if he owned the car. McKenna was impressed.

She didn't tell him. Somehow she felt he expected her to say something. She didn't know if he expected a compliment or some sarcasm. She said nothing instead. But she was impressed. Parker could help with the driving. It was much better than having Lydia along. She didn't drive a clutch and her incessant conversation could drive McKenna batty at times. She'd gotten used to having Parker with her. And it surprised her how fast that transition had taken.

"What are you thinking?" he asked.

She smiled, again feeling caught. "I was thinking about Lydia."

"I'm sure she's fine. By now she's out of the hospital—"

"I wasn't thinking about her leg," she interrupted.

He glanced at her before looking back at the road. "I was thinking that I'm glad you insisted on coming along," she confessed.

His expression changed. His face became a mask, not a hard one, but a mask disguised to conceal the emotions going on behind it. McKenna couldn't tell what was going on in his mind, but she was sure he appreciated the fact that she no longer resented him.

She found he could almost be as stubborn as she was. Strangely, she liked it in a weird sort of way. She hadn't fought with anyone since Marshall and while she and Parker didn't have the same relationship, she felt there was much more to him than she'd previously thought. Sure, he worked on his computer a lot and for long times could be silent, almost oblivious to her presence, but she didn't feel alone.

Alone.

Suddenly that word stuck in her head. She had been alone since Marshall died. She'd filled her days with work, never really allowing herself to think about anything. She'd spent her leisure time with friends and even when she was by herself, she'd always be doing something, reading, going over sales reports, checking inventory, completing emails or preparing for some event she was obligated to attend. And then there was the car. When she began restoring it, it took all her free time. She hadn't yet given in to herself. She didn't know what would happen if she did.

"DID YOU EVER play license tag?" Parker asked as an 18-wheeler roared past them, sucking the air behind the Corvette and pushing the small car slightly sideways. McKenna's grip on the steering wheel kept them steady in the wake. The most traffic they had seen on the road so far was an occasional UPS or FedEx truck. These always quickly turned down a side street, heading for a local delivery. The 18-wheeler took the first turn that headed toward the interstate highway and was soon out of sight.

"It was something to do in the backseat of a car on long trips. Why?" McKenna elongated the word as she glanced his way.

"I was playing it silently, but it might make the miles go by faster if we did it together."

"No proper nouns or slang words," she said, immediately setting down some rules.

"That depends on the game," he paused a moment. "If you play states, they're all proper nouns. If you just play words, then your rules apply. If you play proper nouns only, then you use proper nouns. If you play first and last letter, your rules don't apply."

"Apparently, you've made a study of this game. Did you travel a lot when you were younger?"

"We often went on some kind of driving trip, whether it was in a car or on a bus. My dad took us on vacation every year. We'd play the game as soon as we got on the road."

McKenna saw a glow in his eyes when he talked about his family. She knew nothing about them.

"Do you have siblings?"

"A brother and a sister," he replied. "Neither of them live close by. One is in Washington state. The other in China."

"They sound adventurous." She made the covert contrast about him and his two absent siblings.

"You could say that."

"What do they do?"

"My sister is an engineer in China. On the side, she teaches English to Chinese children. My brother owns a ski lodge, but that's only so he can go mountain climbing every chance he gets."

"It must be fun to have brothers and sisters. I'm an only child. Before my parents died, we used to go on a lot of trips. Some were by car, but most required an airplane."

Parker nodded.

"Alone," McKenna nearly shouted as she pointed at a pickup truck that moved pass them. "The license tag had LON on it."

"So we're not using all the letters on the tag, only three of them?"

"We can use all of them. In that case the non-proper noun using PHE LON is phone line."

"That's two words," Parker said.

"We didn't establish a rule against the number of words."

"So you're going to make up the rules as we go?" he asked.

She smiled at him. "Isn't that more fun?"

"Sort of like this trip?" Parker added. "We go along until we find something interesting?"

"Exactly."

The way he looked at her was disconcerting. McKenna wanted to ask him what he was thinking, but she feared his answer. She didn't know what it would be and didn't understand why she should be afraid of hearing it, but she was.

PARKER SQUINTED INTO the Western sun as he waited for his takeout order. He thought he saw her. He was sure it was the same girl. She was a wily one and always hid or concealed herself when she thought she might be seen. He'd glimpsed her before—twice. And he recognized the signs. If she lived along this part of the route, it would surprise him. But it wasn't likely he would find out.

He and McKenna were leaving in a week. Their lack of cash had slowed them down, but they'd found temporary jobs in a small Missouri factory town to supplement the lost income. McKenna would replace a worker on the floor of a sheet factory. Apparently her previous factory experience had gotten her the job. For an economics professor it wasn't so easy. Parker found a temporary job through an agency with a gardening company. It was back-breaking work, but it paid enough for them to get to the next stop on McKenna's flexible agenda. Like the game they played with the license tags, the agenda changed as often as the road signs.

And that agenda was coming into play soon. The wheel was almost up and they'd be moving on.

A crop of short dark hair that looked as if

it hadn't been combed in months poked out of an orange cap. Despite the weather, she covered herself completely—jeans, a shirt and a jacket, all of which were dirty. The first time Parker had seen her was at the gas station when he was filling the car. Stealthily she'd looked out from the door to the toilet, checking all directions before slipping through the small opening. She moved ghostlike around the side of the building and disappeared from sight. Parker told no one that he'd seen her.

The second time was near the supermarket. It had been a long day and the sun was already set when he and McKenna went to buy salads for their simple dinner. The girl, who looked to be fifteen or younger, went around the back of the building. She had that same sly movement he'd seen earlier. Parker knew she was going to look for discarded and possibly rotting food.

"Would you add a tuna fish sandwich on wheat and a large milk to my order," he told the clerk at the deli counter in the supermarket.

"Really hungry tonight?" McKenna asked, her brows arching upward.

"No," he said.

She looked confused, but at that moment the clerk interrupted them. "What would you like on it?"

Parker considered how lean the girl seemed. "Lettuce, tomatoes, mayo and a pickle on the side."

The clerk worked quickly and in seconds he was packaging their order. Parker asked for a separate bag for the tuna and milk. As they left the supermarket, McKenna looked at him skeptically. They were on a budget, but this was still within their daily allowance.

They went to the car and McKenna got in, placing her food in the small crevice behind the seat. Parker did the same with one bag.

"Got a pen?" he asked.

McKenna searched through her purse and pulled out a marker.

Parker reached for it. "That's better than a pen."

He wrote on the bag. *This is for you.* Handing the marker to her, he started walking back toward the grocery store.

"Parker," McKenna called. "Where are you going?"

"I'll only be a minute."

Parker didn't see the girl. He walked behind the building. Maybe she'd moved on already. He assumed she would be by there again and soon. Placing the bag of food on the lid of a Dumpster, he left and returned to McKenna and the car.

"What was that all about?" she asked as soon as he was seated.

"Have you seen her?" Parker asked.

"Seen who?"

"The little girl. She's a runaway."

McKenna searched around the area. Parker knew she wouldn't see anything or anyone.

"What did you do with the food?"

"I left it for her. Behind the grocery store is a Dumpster. I left it on top for her to find."

"How do you know she's a runaway?"

"She's not the first one I've seen."

Again McKenna looked around them.

"It's warm outside, yet she's wearing a

jacket. Her clothes are dirty, and she uses the gas station to wash up. I've seen her twice near places where there is discarded food."

"That doesn't mean she's a runaway."

"Take my word for it."

McKenna looked at him strangely, but she didn't push further.

"Did she see you leave the food?'

He shook his head.

"How do you know she'll get it?"

"She'll find it," he said decisively. Parker shifted gears and headed for the bed-and-breakfast where they were staying.

THE NEXT MORNING Parker left the girl another serving of food. For dinner, later that same day, he and McKenna went to the grocery store and bought her a bag of food: canned fruit, tins of vegetables and sausages that didn't require cooking. Only the bread and milk were perishable.

They didn't see her, but the food from earlier had disappeared.

"Do you think she's all right?" McKenna asked after they'd left the second bag of groceries and returned to the car.

Parker shook his head. "I don't know."

"We only have a few more days before we leave. What do you think she'll do for food then?"

"The same as she did before. She'll scour Dumpsters and restaurant throw-outs."

"I wonder why she's out here alone," McKenna said, but her comment was directed more to herself than to Parker.

THE MOMENT SHE saw the girl, McKenna knew she was the one. Parker said she was a runaway. McKenna was sure he was right and that the girl was on her own—alone and more than likely in need of someone. "She probably believes we're looking for her and that's why we leave the food," he'd said.

Coming out of the factory, McKenna checked for Parker. He often met her in the parking lot. He was in the usual place, leaning next to the car, his legs crossed at the ankles, his face in a book. If he wasn't typing on his computer, he was reading. As she walked toward him, he looked up and smiled when he saw her. McKenna returned it. They'd fallen into a casual routine and she was glad to see him.

Lifting her arm, she waved and that was when she saw the girl hiding behind a large tree across from the parking lot. McKenna stumbled, but caught herself.

"You're late," Parker said.

McKenna ignored him. His voice was teasing as it usually was when he picked her up. "She's there," McKenna told him.

"She? The girl?" His brows rose and he stood up straight. "Where?" He looked over his shoulder.

"Exactly as you predicted. She's hiding behind a tree on the other side of the road."

Parker started to turn in that direction, but McKenna pulled him back to face her. "Don't look," she whispered as if the girl could hear them. "You might frighten her."

McKenna stepped sideways to go around him. "I think I'll go talk to her." She glanced at Parker. "If she's been abused, as you thought, she'll be more receptive to me."

"Be careful," Parker said.

"Why?"

"She doesn't know your intentions. And she's scared. You don't want to corner her."

McKenna nodded. Approaching the girl too quickly would surely make her run, so McKenna kept her distance. She went about putting her purse and the factory smock she wore over her clothes on the passenger seat. Parker got in the car, but she stood leaning against it and staring at the tree. Cars pulled out of spaces and people waved at her as they headed home for the evening.

McKenna remained in place.

The girl stayed behind the tree. Fear of others was the unknown factor for a runaway. In the girl's eyes McKenna could be someone who'd make more trouble for her, or she could be friendly. The problem was, the girl didn't know which one was the right answer.

The girl's appearance wasn't totally unexpected. Curiosity must have forced her to come and find out. She would be ready to run, probably had an escape plan in place.

The girl peeked out from behind the tree. Quickly, she moved back as she spotted McKenna standing in the same place.

Waiting a full minute, she looked out again. McKenna hadn't moved. This time the girl let herself be seen intentionally. She made eye contact with McKenna, but neither moved toward each other.

McKenna wondered what her reason for running away was. Had she been abused? Where was she from, and how did she get to this part of Route 66? She wondered where the girl slept. Since she used public rest-rooms to wash up, she couldn't have a real place to stay.

"What do you want?" the girl called, star-tling McKenna.

McKenna stood up and took a step for-ward. The girl moved back. McKenna stopped.

"I don't want anything," McKenna hol-lered back.

"Why do you leave the food?"

"Because you're hungry."

"What do you care?"

McKenna turned around and pulled a bag out of the car. She held it up to the girl.

"What's that?" the girl asked. A look of

apprehension went across her face, before it disappeared.

"Do we have to continue shouting? I promise I'm not out to harm you."

"I've heard that before," she yelled over.

McKenna wondered if that was a confirmation that she had been abused. "Is that a yes or a no?"

For a long while, the girl scrutinized McKenna. "You can come," she finally said. "But don't try anything funny. And don't get too close."

McKenna almost laughed. Her words sounded like something out of a movie. She crossed the parking lot and the road and entered the field. The girl looked at McKenna's approach as if she could read something in the way she walked.

"That's far enough," the girl said when McKenna was ten feet from her.

McKenna stopped. "This is for you." She held up the bag. "I'm going to toss it to you." Before the girl could give her alternate instructions, she pitched it.

The girl caught it awkwardly, balancing quickly as the heavy objects inside the plastic bag shifted. Keeping her eyes on McKenna, she briefly checked the contents.

"It's shampoo, lotion, a toothbrush. Nothing that will harm you," McKenna told her.

"Who are you?" She frowned.

"My name's McKenna Wellington. I'm from Chicago."

"And the man? Is he your husband?"

McKenna shook her head. "He's a college professor. We're traveling west to the coast."

McKenna noticed that she spoke very good English. She'd been educated somewhere.

"How old are you?" McKenna asked.

"Why?" The girl's face was straight, serious, but there was a vulnerability there, too.

"Are you a runaway?"

"No, I live a mile from here." Her voice was challenging, laced with sarcasm.

"Why?"

"Why what?" the girl challenged.

"Why did you run away?" McKenna deliberately kept her voice even.

"None of your business."

"Why did you come to find me?"

"I wasn't looking for you. I just happened

to see that car." She gestured with her chin toward the red car in the parking lot.

"It does stand out," McKenna said, not looking around. "Why did you call out to me?"

"I wanted to know why you leave me the food."

McKenna smiled. "Parker got the food." She indicated Parker standing by the car.

"The professor?"

McKenna nodded. "He saw you first."

She almost smiled, but quickly the expression left her face.

"I suppose as a man who often comes in contact with people your age or older, he's been trained to notice the signs."

"I'm not a runaway."

"Let's see," McKenna started. "You wash up in public restrooms. You come to Dumpsters for food. You wear the same clothes day in and day out, including a jacket in this heat. You're afraid of meeting people. You think someone is looking for you. You have no real place to sleep or you'd be able to wash yourself and your clothes. Did I miss something?"

The girl dropped her gaze to the ground, but immediately raised it again. Her jaw took on a challenging stance.

McKenna waited a moment longer for her to reply. "I guess I have my answer," she said. "I'm going now. Parker is waiting for me. We'll leave you some food at the usual place tomorrow. If you want a shower, I can offer you mine, but we're leaving in a few days."

McKenna turned and made her way back to the car without looking at the girl. She figured if she could get the girl to trust her, she had to let her know she was telling the truth.

"DEFINITELY A RUNAWAY," Parker said as McKenna slid into the passenger seat.

"Do you think she'll return?"

He nodded. "It'll take her a day or so, but she'll come. I think she wants someone to talk to. She just hasn't found anyone she trusts yet. But we may be gone by the time she gets around to doing that with us."

McKenna frowned. "I told her we were leaving in a few days."

"She'll show," Parker repeated.

"You sound positive."

"She made first contact. We're the closest thing she has to a lifeline, as far as we know. She'll come before we leave."

"If she doesn't, do you think we can stay a couple more days?"

Parker glanced at her. She couldn't read his expression. They hadn't had this situation before.

"You want to make sure she's all right?"

"I want to try to get her to go home, unless that's where the abuse happened. If it is, we should get her to go to a safe place."

"It'll eat into our funds if we stay longer. We're already feeding her and providing her with personal hygiene products," Parker pointed out.

The cost wasn't much, McKenna knew. Not if they were getting it from their pre-Route 66 days. But their funds now were low and they were very conscious of what they could spend. The girl had become another person to feed and possibly clothe.

"We've already proven we can cope with what we have and what jobs bring us."

"Don't worry," he said, putting his hand on her arm. "We'll stay and make sure she's safe and has a place to stay."

McKenna smiled. The car was small. Parker's hand remained on her arm. He wanted to let her know that he agreed with making sure the girl was safe. But he hadn't taken it away. McKenna felt its weight, the warmth and strength of his hand. Inside, her stomach tightened.

THE ROOM AT THE bed-and-breakfast where McKenna and Parker stayed was huge, with light gray walls and maroon appointments. It also had its own entrance, which was a plus for the rental. No one had visited them since they'd taken the room for the three weeks they'd been in Carthage. Both turned and stared at each other when the unexpected sound of someone approaching seemed to reverberate through the entire room.

Parker's brow rose and McKenna hunched her shoulders. Together they went to the door and peered through the curtain.

"Well, look who it is. Seems you were right," McKenna said.

McKenna pulled the door open. The girl stood there.

"For the owner of a multimillion dollar company, you certainly didn't pick the best side of town to stay in," she said by way of greeting.

McKenna wanted to laugh, but she kept her face straight.

"Would you like to come in?" Parker asked.

The girl hesitated.

McKenna noticed her looking about the room. "It's probably safer in here than out there," she said.

The girl stepped across the threshold. She was carrying a backpack, but in her hand was the plastic bag McKenna had given her this afternoon.

"Did you come for the shower?"

"I came to see if you really are who the internet says you are."

"Internet?" Parker spoke for the first time.

"I went to the library and looked her up. Found you, too."

"Enterprising," he said.

"Why are you here?" the girl asked.

"First things first," McKenna said. "You know our names. We don't know yours."

"Julie West," she said.

The name rolled easily off her tongue, but McKenna knew that wasn't her real name.

"All right," she conceded. "Just so you know, I don't believe that's genuine, but at least we have something to call you."

Julie looked at the floor, then back up.

"What are you doing here?" she asked again. "I don't think you're specifically searching for me."

"So, you are a runaway," McKenna said.

"No, I'm a survivor."

"I see," McKenna said. The look she gave the girl conveyed something else. "Do you want to use the shower first?"

"First?"

"Then we'll talk."

"I didn't come to talk."

McKenna's brows rose. "All right. The shower is through there." She pointed toward the bathroom door. "I'll give you something to put on and we can wash your clothes while you're in there."

McKenna pulled a T-shirt and a pair of

shorts from a drawer and offered them to her. Julie stared at them.

"I promise we'll give you your things back in the same condition, only clean."

The girl took the clothes and went into the bathroom. She kept her backpack with her. Moments later, she slipped her dirty clothes out the door and McKenna heard the lock click before the shower started.

"Why don't I go wash these? You two can talk," Parker offered.

"Where will you be in the meantime?"

"I'll go get a coffee and check the internet and see if I can find a Julie West." Parker smiled and took the clothes and his computer.

Julie spent a long time in the shower. McKenna figured it had been a while since she could wash her whole body. When she came out, she was wearing the clothes which were too large for her slight frame. It was obvious she wasn't eating regularly. Even though McKenna didn't know her, she could tell she should weigh more.

Her hair was blond, the dirt and grime rinsed away by the shampoo. She'd brushed it away from her face, which was devoid of makeup and shining clean. It showed a girl on the verge of womanhood.

"Are we alone?" she asked.

"Parker went for coffee. He felt you'd be more comfortable without his presence."

She shrugged as if it didn't matter to her.

"He's a college professor and he's looking out for your welfare..."

"I don't need anyone to look out for me."

"All right," McKenna said, choosing not to fight. "There are some snacks and drinks on the table. Help yourself."

Julie checked the table first before getting a soft drink. They had no milk, which they'd been leaving for her. She also took a box of cookies but did not eat them. McKenna assumed she'd stockpile them for later.

She took a seat in a chair near the door.

"We're going to be here awhile," McKenna said. "At least until your clothes dry. Are you going to just sit and stare for all that time?"

"Why are you staying here?" The girl asked.

"The price was right."

"You got all the money in the world and…" She looked around. The room was clean, but old. The furnishings showed their age, but they were sturdily built. "Why would you stay in a place like this?"

"What's wrong with it? It's clean. We get a free breakfast. It's convenient to our jobs. What's not to like?"

"You do know this is not the best part of town."

"You said that. Yet you're living in worse conditions than we are."

"You don't know where I live."

"I don't have to. I know how you clean up, so I assume you sleep outside. What happens when the weather changes? Where will you get food when we leave?"

Julie took a sip from her drink. "Don't worry about me. I'll be fine."

"I do worry about you," McKenna told her.

"Why? You don't know me."

"That's right. I've shared my food with you, shared my bathroom and for the moment provided safety."

"You want something in return?" The belligerence was back.

"No, but what happens to you when the police pick you up? And they will."

"Not if I don't do anything illegal."

"You don't have to. There's probably a missing persons report out on you. And if we discovered your habits, surely someone else will in a town this small."

"I'm careful."

"We discovered you." McKenna delivered the words softly, giving them more impact than if she'd shouted.

Julie looked down, then took another drink.

"What's wrong with home?" McKenna asked, again using the same soft voice.

Her head snapped up and she glared at McKenna. "I don't have a home."

"Did anyone hurt you there?"

"I wasn't abused."

"Just like you're not a runaway?"

For a long moment, the girl stared at her. McKenna held her eyes steady and let her look.

"I didn't have a soft life like you, but I'm not here because someone tried to rape me."

"That's good to hear." McKenna paused. "How old are you? Fifteen? Sixteen?"

"I'm old enough."

"For what?" McKenna asked. "To have found me on the internet and believe I had a cushioned life. And that makes you angry with the world because your life is different?"

"I didn't say that."

"Didn't you?" McKenna took a seat opposite Julie. "Okay. Even if you didn't, just what kind of life did you have, Julie? One in which you ran away, live on the streets and hunt for food. You chose that. Nobody forced it on you."

She sat up in her chair. "What do you know about it?"

"Nothing. Why don't you tell me?"

The air in the room was thick with anger. McKenna took a deep breath.

"I apologize," she said. "I know nothing about your life and all you know about mine is what's in my company bio. You've used the shower. Parker will be back with your clothes soon. You can leave and follow whatever life you choose for yourself. We're leaving shortly anyway."

McKenna got up and took her purse from

the desk. She and Parker had very little money, but she was willing to part with some of it for the girl. She and Parker could get to the next town and find work. She took out several bills and went to the chair where the girl sat.

"I don't need that." Julie said.

"We've argued enough tonight. Take the money." McKenna put it on the window ledge next to her chair and went back to her own seat.

"She got married," the girl mumbled, just loud enough for McKenna to hear her.

McKenna turned around. "Your mother?" Julie nodded.

"And you don't like her husband?"

"Not exactly."

"What is it, exactly?"

"It was supposed to be just us. Just the two of us."

"Was that what you two promised each other when your father…" She left the question hanging, unsure if the father had died, left, or the couple divorced.

"He died," she filled the answer in for McKenna.

"I'm sorry. Obviously, you and your father were close."

She looked up. For a split second, McKenna saw her eyes mist. She blinked and it was gone.

"We were. But he got sick."

"What happened?" McKenna thought Julie's father had to have been a relatively young man. Julie was a teenager. When McKenna was her age, her father was in his forties. Women married later and had children later, but even if he was in his fifties, that was young, too.

"They said it was an aneurysm in his brain. He was fine one minute and the next he was gone."

"When was that?"

"Five months ago."

Five months, McKenna thought. Then it hit her. Julie's father had barely died before her mother remarried. The girl was still grieving. No wonder she was angry.

"I'm so sorry, Julie."

"It's all right. I'm…"

"You don't," McKenna said when the girl had stopped speaking. "You accept it.

You learn to live with it. But you never get over it." McKenna's parents were both gone. She had lost them when she was in college. Lucky for her, they had provided for her welfare. Though not rich, her life in that sense hadn't been affected significantly. But she understood how Julie felt. "Did you run away because your mother remarried?"

"They didn't need me there. And they didn't want me." Tears clogged her voice.

"Are you sure?"

"Of course, I'm sure." The tears were replaced with teenage belligerence. "They—"

At that point the door opened and Parker stood there. McKenna checked Julie's reaction, but her own was the more surprising. Julie only looked at him as a familiar stranger. McKenna felt her heart skip a beat.

"May I come in?" he asked.

"Sure," Julie said. "The more the merrier."

Parker closed the door and went to Julie. He held his laptop in one hand and extended his other to her. "Hello, Joanna. I'm Parker Fordum."

Which one of them was the more surprised wasn't evident. "Where are my clothes?" Julie asked.

"The dryer is still running," Parker said. Julie didn't accept his hand and he dropped it, then moved to sit next to McKenna on the edge of the twin bed. "McKenna, meet Joanna Marie Pearson of Cedar Creek, Arkansas."

"How did you find out?" Julie or Joanna asked.

"I'm good with the computer, too. Finding you was only a matter of adding the elements I knew about you to the missing persons database."

Joanna rose. "Then my mom…"

Parker put his hand out to stop her. "I didn't call her. I think you should do that. She's distraught with worry, from what I saw of the news reports that said they're searching for you."

Joanna resumed her seat. "She doesn't care about me. She probably only reported me missing because I'm a minor and she'd get put in jail if she didn't."

"Joanna," McKenna used her real name for the first time. "You were smart enough to find out about me on the internet. You thought your mother had sent someone to find you. But did you never check to see if they were actually looking for you? You're obviously intelligent enough to do an internet search. Didn't you ever try to find out?"

Joanna looked embarrassed. "I didn't want to see her. There were times I started to look, but I'd close the program and leave the library or wherever I found internet service."

Parker got up and put his computer on the small table where he and McKenna often shared their evening meal. They'd cleared the food away earlier and left only their snacks and drinks and a couple of books.

He looked at Joanna, silently offering her an invitation to use it.

"We'll leave you alone for a few minutes. All you need to do is open the laptop."

Parker extended his arm toward McKenna. She stood and walked into his embrace. It wasn't planned, but it felt right, natural, as if this was what she should do, where she should be.

They moved toward the door, but McKenna

stopped. She turned to Joanna, who hadn't moved from her spot by the window, although her expression was full of pain and she seemed sadder than she had when she'd first come in.

"If you decide to call, feel free to use the phone."

"And remember, they were looking for you," Parker added.

He reached for McKenna again. She took his hand and the two of them left the room. It was a warm night, with a full moon. The porch of the B&B had a bench and they sat on it.

"How did you find out who she was so quickly?" McKenna asked.

"Missing persons is a matter of public record. I used her description, age range and figured she had to be from somewhere nearby. Since she's on foot, or a possible hitchhiker, she couldn't be that far from her home state. Plus she probably hadn't resorted to stealing yet, given her Dumpster visits."

"How did that help?"

"The longer she would have been on the

road, the more likely she'd try stealing food when she couldn't find any."

"And that's why you started buying the food?"

"I didn't want her arrested. She'd be forced back home then, and I wasn't sure that she wasn't an abused child."

He wouldn't want her back in a bad situation. McKenna made a mental note to ask about that later. She felt this wasn't Parker's first experience with a homeless child.

"What else did you do to find her real name?"

"I checked the four states around this one. When I didn't find her, I added another four to the criteria. And there she was. Then I went to the news reports. I listened to the mother ask for information. She appeared genuine. What did she tell you?"

"She said her father died five months ago and her mother is already remarried. She's hurt, grieving and angry."

Parker nodded. "I understand." He was quiet for a moment. "I read the newspaper accounts and the messages people left about her father's death. According to them, he was a wonderful man. And he loved his daughter."

"What about the wife?"

"She seems to be way in the background. There's almost nothing on her. There are accounts of sporting events Joanna took part in, mostly swimming, photos of father and daughter at various school activities, but nothing of the mother."

"Maybe the mother was the photographer or she's camera shy."

"I thought of that. You know how everything is credited these days. I checked the photo credits. None of them were hers. In the narratives and posted stories, there was little to nothing about her."

"I wonder why Joanna is so upset that she remarried."

"She was replacing Joanna's father, whom she obviously loved."

From around the corner of the porch, the young girl appeared. McKenna stood up and took a step toward her.

"How did it go?" she asked.

Joanna turned to her. Her bottom lip trembled. Tears were in her eyes. She shook her head from side to side, as if she was trying to shake away the answer. Without a word, she stumbled off the porch and ran out into the night as if the devil were on her heels.

"I wish we could do more," Parker said, coming up behind McKenna. He put his hands on her shoulders and pulled her back against him. "I feel terrible for her. I thought for sure things would have worked out for them."

"Parker," she said. "I have the feeling we've made a terrible mistake."

CHAPTER SIX

MCKENNA WAS SLUGGISH when she got out of bed the next morning. She'd been awake most of the night. She couldn't get Joanna out of her mind. The look on the young girl's face when she appeared on the porch haunted her. Had they done the right thing for Joanna? McKenna wanted to go after her, but Parker's logic that it was dark and that Joanna had a hiding place kept McKenna at the B&B.

Work the next day went by slowly. At every break, McKenna went outside looking for Joanna. She couldn't find her. The tree where she'd hidden yesterday showed no sign of her. McKenna checked the entire area, but Joanna was not there.

When the day ended, she hoped Joanna would show up to collect the food Parker had left for her. She and Parker went into the diner they'd started frequenting and ordered. It was close enough to the supermarket for them to see anyone going that way.

"How are you feeling?" he asked after the waitress left them.

"Like a criminal."

"You didn't do anything illegal."

"I know. But I feel like I let her down. That we were on the right track, but it was in fact wrong."

"It wasn't," Parker said.

"How do you know?"

Parker glanced around before saying anything. "She's a survivor. She'll come around. She needed time to process everything we said." He paused as the waitress delivered their food. Tonight they'd opted to eat in the diner instead of buying the food and taking it back to their room. "Kids on the street are a different breed. Some of them learn things long before they should. Joanna's been gone for months. In our eyes, that's not a long time, but for someone who's actually living that life, three months is a lifetime."

"You think she's ready to go home?" McKenna surmised.

"I do."

McKenna glanced out the window, hoping she'd see the young girl. A couple of pick-up trucks roared down the road, but no pedestrian materialized.

"She didn't call anyone."

McKenna looked at him in surprise. She waited for him to explain.

"I checked with the desk," he told her. "No phone calls were made from our room. She did watch the news reports on the laptop. All the windows were left open on the screen."

"What are we going to do now?"

Parker reached over and took her hand. McKenna felt that jolt of awareness again.

"It's up to her," he said. "We opened the door. It's up to her to walk through it."

They lingered over dinner for an hour. McKenna continually checked the window, but she never spotted Joanna. When they left, the bag of food still sat in its usual place behind the diner. McKenna's heart dropped again when she saw it. Parker took her hand and led her to the car.

"We'll only be here two more days. I feel like we'll be leaving something undone."

"It's not over yet," he assured her.

It wasn't that McKenna wasn't aware of Parker's touch. She was super aware of it. He'd done it more than once. At first she'd excused her reaction as the fact that it had been a long time since a man had touched her. But now that he had held her hand, put his arm around her shoulders and pulled her against him, she felt a real connection to him.

It confused her. She was with Parker, not her husband, not the man she'd vowed to love until her dying day. How could this be? Parker was all but responsible for Marshall's death. He'd been there with him. Been the help he needed, yet Marshall had died. McKenna had to be losing her mind. Of course, she was worried about Joanna, but that was no reason to allow Parker to hold her in a romantic way. And certainly no reason that she should like it.

McKenna didn't have time to dwell on her feelings for Parker. As he pulled the car into the lot at the B&B, Joanna was there waiting for them. She sat on the steps leading to their room as if she hadn't a care in the world. She was clean, wearing a white T-shirt and pink shorts. Next to her sat a paper bag.

McKenna was out of the Corvette before the moment Parker stopped the car. She ran to the girl. Joanna stood up as she approached. Without thinking, McKenna grabbed her in a bear hug.

"Is everything all right?" McKenna asked. She pushed back, eyeing her up and down as if to assure herself that Joanna had all her fingers and toes. Parker came up behind her.

Joanna nodded, and seemed a little taken aback by McKenna's affection. "Sorry about last night. I wasn't ready to see and hear all those things on his computer."

Joanna dropped her chin and McKenna gave her a moment.

The girl looked down and picked up the bag. "Your clothes," she said.

McKenna took the bag and they led her into the small room they shared, a family reunited after a long absence. Parker took a seat at the table. McKenna sat poised on the end of one of the beds. Joanna perched on the guest chair.

"Did you believe them?" Parker asked,

"Yeah. My mom was crying. I started to cry."

McKenna saw the emotion cover her face. Tears welled in the girl's eyes, even though she fought to blink them away.

"What about her husband?" Parker asked.

"I'm okay with him."

"Are you sure?" McKenna needed to know.

Joanna nodded. "Last night I thought about how things were before my father died. They weren't that great." She paused and swallowed as if she had to force the words out. "My mom and dad fought a lot. I could hear them, even if they didn't think I could. When we were together, they talked to me or through me, not to each other. I can't blame my mom or him for falling in love."

"That's very mature," Parker said. McKenna glanced at him to see if there was any sarcasm in his meaning. She found none.

"But you didn't call them," Parker stated.

It wasn't a question, but she answered it anyway. "I'm afraid," she admitted. "I figured if I just go there I can see if they'll welcome me. I bought a bus ticket with the money you gave me." She looked at McKenna. Parker followed her gaze.

"Of course they'll welcome you," McKenna said.

"You should give them a call," Parker advised. "Stop them from worrying."

"I don't know what to say. "

"That's easy," McKenna told her with a smile. "Start with 'I love you.'"

She wasn't sure why she looked at Parker as she said that. He was staring at her. Maybe she sensed herself being looked at. Or maybe she looked at him for approval. Whatever it was, the air between them seemed to take on a charge.

"Your parents will take it from there," Parker said.

Parker stood up, indicating the phone. He and McKenna went to the door, giving Joanna time alone to call her parents. Just before the door closed, McKenna heard her dialing the phone.

THEY WERE ON the road again. Parker's heart was lighter. McKenna practically glowed. He liked to see her happy. She wore her hair down this morning. The wind tossed it back and forth and occasionally she'd put her hand up and push it out of her face. She was brunette. Her shoulder-length curly hair was shining with copper highlights in the sun. It complemented her brown eyes.

"You look like the cat that ate the canary."

McKenna grinned. Together they had taken Joanna to the bus station and watched and waved as she'd boarded the bus and it drove away. The smile on Joanna's face was teary, but Parker felt she was going to be all right. He'd seen many students in her predicament. Maybe not so drastic, not too many runaways, but enough that he knew the signs when he saw them. And the signs of recovery.

"How much money did you give her?" Parker asked.

McKenna looked at him, her brows raised.

"I saw you," he explained.

"After we got her some new clothes, I gave her enough to buy food until she gets back to Cedar Creek and a little extra."

"You mean all you had left in your wallet?" Parker asked.

"Not all, but most," she said, dipping her head.

Parker laughed at her.

"She needed it, and we can survive."

"Don't feel bad about it. I did the same thing," Parker told her.

"You gave her money?"

He nodded. "She told me you had already given her some, but I wanted to make sure if she decided to take a few days to get home, she wouldn't be sleeping on the streets."

McKenna put her hand on his arm. It was the first time she'd touched him. The electricity that radiated through him made him swerve the car. Quickly he compensated, hoping McKenna didn't notice.

She dropped her hand and shifted in the passenger seat.

"You know, you broke your own rule," Parker spoke up, needing to do something to break the tension that coiled inside him.

"Rule? What rule?"

"The one about email and cell phones."

"I haven't used either," she defended.

"But you have to now."

"Why?"

"You gave Joanna your email address and phone number and told her to get in touch with you if she needed anything."

"So?"

"So, now you have to check it to see if she sends a message or calls." Parker shrugged. "If she sends you a message, and I'm sure she will when she gets home, you'll have to answer her, even if it's only to be courteous."

Parker laughed again and McKenna joined in, however her expression said something else. "What?" Parker asked, frowning.

"I didn't break the rule."

"I saw you writing down the information."

"It wasn't *my* information," McKenna said.

"Whose..." He stopped as understanding dawned. "You didn't?"

"Well, it's your computer. You're always writing on it or looking something up. I thought it only fair that she be able to reach us and since I'm never on the machine, you were the obvious choice."

Parker smiled wide. "You are certainly a card, McKenna. You have all the bases covered."

For a few moments they rode in silence. Then McKenna turned in her seat and faced him. He was getting used to the subtle way she acted. She had something important to say and even though they were in the car, she wanted his full attention.

"I've been thinking," she began.

"Is that a dangerous thing to do?" Parker joked. He liked joking with her, liked to see her let her guard down. He got glimpses of the real McKenna then.

"In the towns we stop in, even if we don't need the money, why don't we stay a few days, get jobs, meet some of the people who live along this route."

"Instead of just letting the scenery pass us by?"

"Exactly," she said. Her face glowed as if she was a child getting a gift.

"Well, we could always use the money. And you wanted to see some of the sights."

"You could use some of our experiences for a future book. You don't only write economics textbooks, do you?"

"So far that's all I've written."

"But I see you typing new stuff in your computer. I thought you only had to edit your book. Are you adding new material at the same time?"

"Not exactly," he said, all noncommittal.

"Are you keeping notes about this trip?"

He was. He was keeping both notes and impressions of the places they had been. He wasn't thinking of writing a book. He told himself when he started that he only wanted to document the trip so he could remember it later. But he knew what he really wanted to remember later were details related to McKenna. She would never forgive him for his part in Marshall's death. When they returned to Chicago, he was sure they would each resume their separate lives.

"That was always the plan," she continued. "To stop and see the area, visit some of the local places, work along the way and meet new people."

"Is this because of Joanna?"

"A little. I felt I was doing something positive, maybe even life changing. Not just giving her a handout and passing her by."

"Are you saying you want to try solving people's problems?"

"No," she said. "I just think it's a shame to

drive across the country and not meet some people along the way."

"I see. So you're naturally friendly. It's probably all that sales training coming through," he teased.

"Not necessarily."

McKenna had worked in sales for a long time. When she and Marshall opened their first store, she was the face of the business. A few men tested her, but she proved herself. And most became her friends. McKenna was a natural people person. Marshall couldn't have picked a better salesperson for their business if he'd gotten a Hollywood star to fill the position. Luckily, they couldn't afford to hire anyone in the beginning.

Parker understood where she was coming from. He also understood that, whether he agreed or not, they were going to do it her way.

Two days later, Joanna left an email message for McKenna and Parker. She included a phone number and said she was happy to be home and that she would keep in touch.

As she and Parker neared the Oklahoma state line, McKenna was still thinking about

Joanna. She wondered if there was another email from her, but refused to ask Parker to check. Surely Parker would tell her if he'd discovered there was mail.

McKenna brought her attention back to the road. She pulled the car into a gas station with a diner attached. They'd seen many of these on their trip so far. The gas stations were often old, but most sported new self-service pumps. It was breakfast time and her stomach was telling her it was time to eat.

Getting out of the car, she stretched her back. Looking around, she noticed the land had become very flat. Used to seeing high-rises in Chicago, the buildings around her were mainly two-story offices and other smaller businesses.

"Why don't you go get a table?" Parker suggested. "I'll fill the tank."

Nodding, she saw the lot was full of cars and trucks. McKenna halted on the threshold of the diner. From the outside, the place looked as if it was held together by a wing and a prayer. But the food must be good, because as McKenna stepped through the entrance she saw there was only one empty table in the place. Curious eyes followed her. She sat down, pulling the stained menu from between a napkin holder and an old table-top jukebox.

Ten minutes after she sat down, no one had come to take her order or offer her coffee. McKenna kept her eyes on the room. There was no waitress. A woman came out of the kitchen, dropped a few plates at two tables and rushed back the same way she had come.

McKenna understood. The place was shorthanded. Maybe someone was ill or had quit. In any case, the place was a one-woman show. McKenna smiled. She stood up. The bell over the door rang, indicating new customers arriving. McKenna noted the couple standing in the doorway, the sun behind them casting a silhouette.

"There's a free table right here," she said as if she was the maitre'd.

She didn't wait for them to take seats, but headed for the door marked Employees Only. Inside on the facing wall were several hooks holding aprons. Above them was a table map for the diner. McKenna took a moment to study it before grabbing the cleanest apron and tying it on. She walked toward the sound of sizzling bacon and frying eggs.

The woman glanced up at her as she approached.

"You cook it. I'll serve it," McKenna said, washing her hands.

The woman stared dumbfounded as McKenna quickly scanned the order ticker and stacked three plates along her left arm and took two in her right hand. Backing out the door, applause greeted her. Finding the correct tables, she served the customers their food.

Parker entered as she set the last plate down and headed to the kitchen for more. He stood gaping at her with a confused look on his face.

"Miss, may I have more coffee?" someone said as she passed a table.

"Sure," McKenna answered. Then to Parker, she murmured. "Go wash your hands, grab a pot of coffee and fill every cup in the place."

"I won't ask why," he said.

"Later," she told him. "Right now, we need all the hands we can get."

Without argument, Parker followed her instructions. He was back on the floor as she came out with the second set of plates. When customers left, Parker manned the computerized cash register. The two of them took orders and dished out breakfasts as if they did this on a daily basis. The truth was McKenna hadn't waited tables since she was in college. But, she learned, that once a waitress, the skills were only dormant. They remain ready for reconstitution whenever necessary. And today they had been called into action.

The morning rush ended at 10:30.

"I don't know where you came from, but I never look a gift horse in the mouth." Both McKenna and Parker observed the woman who'd emerged from the kitchen. She'd taken a moment to restore her hair and wipe the shine from her face. She was average height, wearing tennis shoes, khaki pants and a sleeveless purple top. Her shoulder-length brown hair was pulled into a knot on the top of her head and covered with a hairnet. She wore lipstick that might have been fresh when she'd started the day, but she'd eaten it off to the point that only a thin line outlined her mouth.

"Hungry?" the woman asked.

"Starving," Parker said.

"I can't thank you enough. I don't know what I would have done if you hadn't shown up and taken charge. I didn't have time to conduct interviews, cook, serve *and* be the cashier. So, what are your names?"

"McKenna Wellington and Parker Fordum." McKenna glanced toward Parker.

The woman offered her hand. "Sherry Granger," she said.

"What happened?" Parker asked.

"My daughter was coming out to help me, but something came up and she can't get here for a week. My waitress is on maternity leave. The baby was born early this morning, three weeks ahead of schedule. I have a backup, but she's out of town for another week."

"Murphy's Law," Parker said.

The woman nodded.

"Are you the owner?" McKenna asked.

"Lock, stock and two barrels," she quipped. "Are you two staying around here?"

"We're on our way to California," McKenna explained.

"We came for gas and food," Parker added.

"You've obviously worked as a waitress before, and you took to the cash register as if you'd worked it from day one. If you're not in an all-out hurry, could you stick around for a week?"

Parker and McKenna looked at each other. Their luck appeared to have changed. "Are you offering each of us a job?" McKenna asked.

"I know it's temporary and I can't pay you much." She mentioned an hourly rate that should have insulted them both, but McKenna was grateful for it.

"Of course, you can keep all the tips you make." She sweetened the offer, looking questioningly between the two of them. "This sure would help me out."

"Don't you want references or something?"

"If you'd planned to rob me, you had every opportunity. And I'm desperate. I can't afford to close or lose the customers I have. This is my livelihood." She looked around. "It's not much, but it's mine."

"Deal," McKenna said, offering her a wide smile.

"Great," she smiled, too. "Lunch starts at eleven o'clock. We're really busy from eleven-thirty till two. After that we have a reprieve until dinner, and that starts at four-thirty and ends about eight. We clean up and close at nine. It's a long day, but if you're up to it, you'll save my butt."

McKenna looked at Parker and then they both nodded.

"Great. Now, how about some breakfast?"

BY THE TIME the last dish was washed and placed in the cabinet, when the last machine had been cleaned and sanitized, when the floors had been swept and washed and all the salt and pepper shakers filled, McKenna was exhausted. She groaned as she stumbled into the room she and Parker had secured between lunch and dinner. Dropping her purse on a chair, she collapsed facedown on her bed. Every muscle in her body screamed for attention. She hadn't worked as hard as she had today since she and Marshall had spent twenty-four-hour days getting their business off the ground. But back then she'd been right out of college. That was a decade ago and the muscles she'd used then had long since refused the call to action.

Parker had moved their meager possessions into an ancient boardinghouse Sherry had told them about. McKenna had carried her clothes in the canvas bag that the robber had left unscarred.

Since she and Parker were going to be here for at least the next seven days, she didn't want to spend them in a motel. Other than the safety factor, which still bothered her, they had to be careful of their finances. After that first bumpy night, things appeared to be on solid ground ever since. They had jobs again and a secure place to stay.

"Tired?" Parker asked.

"I don't think I can move," she said, her voice muffled into the covers. Raising her head to speak was too much of an effort. And her neck muscles would surely protest.

"I haven't worked like that in years."

McKenna opened an eye and spied him. He sat on the twin bed next to hers.

"You don't look very tired," she said.

"I'm used to being on my feet for twelve hours a day."

McKenna closed her eyes. She wouldn't have thought it. He sat so often, typing on his computer. He looked natural in a chair. She wondered what he would be like in a classroom. She thought of moving, getting up and showering, washing the smell of the diner grease from her hair and clothes, but the effort seemed too much. She'd wait a minute, then get up.

"You'd think, after the sheet factory, that I'd be more in shape," she said. "But most of my time was spent in the office."

Parker moved. She felt his presence shift, although she didn't open her eyes. She thought he was headed for the bathroom. She'd have to wait, but that was fine, since moving required a herculean effort she was not willing to work at. Then she felt his weight anchor her bed down. She jerked up, twisting around to see what he was doing.

"It's all right," he whispered, soothing her.

Gently he removed her shoes and began massaging her feet. Her eyes fluttered closed at the feel of his hands. They were large and sure, warm to the touch. The warmth spread from her toes up her legs. It felt wonderful. Tension left her body as she relaxed and gave herself up to his ministrations. Sensations, delicious and otherwise amazing, overtook her.

McKenna said nothing. She allowed his fingers to work the tiredness from her feet and legs. His thumbs bore into the pad of her foot, circling the skin over and over, and willing fatigue to flee. She kept her eyes closed. Relaxation spread over her and sleep was on its way. Parker removed his hands and stood up. McKenna came awake, although she was drowsy. Taking a few deep breaths, she pushed herself up on her knees.

"Your turn," she said, hoping he didn't hear the tiredness in her voice.

"My turn for what?" Parker asked.

"Foot massage."

"My feet are fine," Parker said.

"Then turn around. I'll massage your

back. I saw you stretching it several times tonight."

He started to say something, but McKenna used one finger and made a spinning gesture for him to turn around. Parker did so. Giving up, he sat on the bottom of the bed. From behind him, McKenna began to knead his muscles. She worked quickly down the hard landscape of his back. Just as she'd done, he moaned quietly, expressing the pleasure of having tension leave his body.

She continued for ten minutes, coming awake with each press of snarled muscle. She'd been dead tired, but after Parker worked on her feet and legs and she on his back, her adrenaline was pumping and she was gaining a second wind. Finishing at his shoulders, she patted them lightly and stepped off the bed.

"I'm going to shower," she told him. Grabbing her still packed bag, she escaped to the bathroom.

Maybe sharing wasn't the best option for them, McKenna told herself as she leaned her back against the door. What was wrong with her? What was happening to her and when had it started? Why was she liking him so much? His hands on her feet had felt so good. He seemed to know exactly what she needed when she needed it. That's something even Marshall had never really figured out. So how could Parker? How could a man she didn't really like make her feel like…what?

McKenna pushed away from the door at the same time she pushed those thoughts far away from her mind, never to be retrieved again.

CHAPTER SEVEN

HE'D GONE TOO FAR, too fast, Parker told himself. He should never have touched her. She looked so tired. He only wanted to help her feel better. But things had gotten out of hand. He'd quit rubbing her feet when he realized he wanted to hold her.

Then she'd put her hands on his back.

Her fingers were sure and efficient, and for a while he thought that she was thinking of him and not Marshall. That he was more than her traveling partner. They were finally on friendly terms, but now he wanted more than that.

Had she sensed it?

He listened to the water in the shower. She'd been in there awhile. Was she all right? It had been a long day and she'd practically fallen asleep as he massaged her feet. Parker didn't know if he should check on her or not. He was usually a decisive man, but with McKenna he was often tongue-tied, especially when he let his feelings take control. In her presence, he held them tightly in check, but tonight he'd let them loose a bit.

The bathroom door opened and out came that fragrance Parker associated with her. McKenna stepped forward. She was wearing the long T-shirt that reached her knees. Her face was freshly washed and free of makeup. Her hair hung in wet tendrils around her face and down her back. She was radiant.

"Feel better?" he asked, noticing his voice was only slightly less tight than earlier.

"Like I had ten pounds of grease and grime washed away."

"I'll go and see if the same thing happens to me." Quickly, he darted toward the bathroom, but not before the scent of her accosted him. It was there in the bathroom, too, as fresh and sensual as if she were standing right next to him.

He turned the water on and removed his shirt when there was a knock on the door. McKenna said something, but he didn't hear it over the sound of the shower and the beating of his own heart. He opened the door.

"What did you say?"

She stood directly outside. She took a step back as if he was too close. Her mouth opened, but she said nothing. Then she swallowed.

"I left my brush. I need it."

He turned and looked at the counter. Several of her things were neatly arranged there. Her toothbrush, toothpaste, comb and brush, deodorant, shampoo. He gestured for her to get what she needed.

McKenna didn't move for a beat, then she hurried past him and into the small room. Taking her comb and brush, he gave her ample space. Parker let out a breath as he closed the door again. He stepped into the shower, making the water temperature colder.

Parker stayed in there longer than necessary. He hoped McKenna would be finished brushing her hair and asleep by the time he left the bathroom. She'd been so tired just a short while ago. She had to be asleep by now.

Opening the door, he saw the lights were

still on. She sat propped up in bed reading. Her hair was still down around her shoulders, although it was nearly dry.

"Did you drop the ten pounds?" she asked, looking up as he came out.

For a moment he didn't connect with what she meant. Then he remembered her comment when she'd returned from her shower.

"At least ten," he said. "I expected you to be asleep by now."

Putting her book aside, she said, "I was tired, but after the shower, I feel a lot better. And my feet are no longer in distress." She wiggled her toes.

Parker's eyes watched her and for an instant he remembered the feel of having her close. He wore blue pajamas, something he hadn't even owned until this trip. After that night when they'd decided they could only afford one room, he knew his usual sleeping attire, or lack of it, was not an option.

Sitting on his single bed, he faced McKenna. "Is this arrangement working, McKenna?"

"What arrangement?"

"This." He spread his hands. "The one

room. We've been fortunate to find pretty decent-paying jobs. Despite the money we gave Joanna, we can afford separate rooms."

She swung her feet to the floor and turned toward him. "Oh."

"Don't you want your own privacy? I know the break-in was a little traumatic, but you're no wilting flower."

"I suppose we should consider it," McKenna said. "I hadn't thought about separate rooms since we lost the money. Initially it was strange having a man in my bedroom who wasn't Marshall."

"But," he prompted.

"But I adapted."

"Just a few minutes ago, when you came into the bathroom for your brush." He glanced at her brush lying on the night stand between the two beds. "You were a little…" He searched for a word. "Aware."

She swallowed and Parker could see a tiny pulse in her neck accelerating. "I've never seen you without a shirt," she said, obviously reaching for a quick answer.

"We both know I'm not the first man you've seen without a shirt."

McKenna glanced down at her fingers which were linked together. "It was the whole thing. The bathroom. You getting into the shower. For a moment it reminded me of Marshall. We used to bump into each other every morning trying to get dressed in the same bathroom. That was before we moved to the new house."

Parker went numb. Her words couldn't have hurt more. Marshall had died three years ago. He should have realized McKenna was still mourning him.

"I'm sorry, Parker."

"It's all right."

"Damn it, stop being so agreeable. You should be angry, slinging words at me. Doing something."

He stared hard at her. "What would you like me to say or do?"

"I don't know. But don't just sit there."

"I am doing something."

"What?"

"I'm keeping my hands off you."

FRIENDSHIP WAS SUCH a fleeting thing. Parker had only just cracked the shell McKenna had built around herself and now they were further apart than they had ever been. He shouldn't have said what he did, but it needed to be said. Maybe not at that moment, but he was tired of carrying around his feelings for her and her not knowing it.

However, since she did know, he'd rendered her silent. McKenna sat, stunned. She'd opened her mouth to speak, but closed it each time. He watched her closely, wondering what she was thinking. Did she have any feelings for him? Deep down inside her was there anything more than friendliness for him?

"Parker," she said, her voice strained as if she had a sore throat and the effort to speak was tremendous. "We're both very tired. It's been a long, long day. We should get some sleep and talk about this in the morning."

Neither of them moved.

"You mean we *don't* talk about this in the morning."

"What?"

She frowned and Parker thought she'd honestly forgotten. "We have to be at the restaurant at five o'clock. There won't be

time to talk in the morning." At least not
the kind of talking he felt they should have.

"Then we'll talk after we finish up tomorrow night."

McKenna stood up then and climbed into
bed. Parker slipped into his own bed. He
folded his frame into what he considered
to be no larger than a cot, with his back to
McKenna. Likewise, she had her back to
him. Parker was sure neither of them slept.
He'd become used to her nighttime habits.
More than once he'd spent the night listening to her breathing, watching her as she
turned and resettled herself. He knew how
she pulled the covers up to her neck and
how she unconsciously pushed her hair back
from her face.

But tonight she was doing none of those
things. Her body was stiff and unmoving,
just as his was. Parker closed his eyes and
waited for sleep to claim him. At 1:00 a.m.
he was still awake. Shifting positions, he
tried to find a comfortable place to relax,
but it wasn't discomfort that was keeping
him awake. It was McKenna. She still had
her back to him.

He closed his eyes and when he opened them, he had the feeling that time had passed. Checking the lit dial on his watch, it read 3:07 a.m. He had barely an hour to sleep before they both needed to get up and get ready for a day of working together. He didn't know how that was going to go. Or how tonight was going to be when they returned to this room and had their talk.

McKenna sat up and faced him. The light mounted outside the door cast a dim glow through the drapes and reflected across her face. Her eyes were wide open. They stared directly into his.

"I didn't sleep well, either," he said.

"What time is it?"

"A little after three."

She moaned and closed her eyes, flopping back down on the bed she pulled her blanket up to her ears. Parker continued to stare at her. After a minute, she opened her eyes.

"What?" she said, sounding defeated.

Parker pushed his covers back and sat up on the side of the bed. He didn't switch on the lamp. His body blocked the light that had been coming through the window. It was probably easier this way, to say what he needed to without seeing her.

"I didn't mean to upset you earlier." He heard her sigh, but went on before she could respond. "I know it came as a surprise to you."

"Not totally," she said.

Parker caught himself from gasping at the last moment.

"You're not the first man who's looked at me. I know the signs."

"But you don't return them." It was a bald fact, an observation he knew to be true.

McKenna pushed herself up in bed and sat back against the headboard. "I'm sorry, Parker. We both know there can't be anything between us."

"Because of Marshall?" he asked.

"Because of Marshall," she repeated.

THE STRAIN ONLY grew worse with the rising of the sun. They tiptoed around each other, being polite but not friendly.

As they got into the car to drive the short distance to the restaurant, McKenna finally spoke.

"Let's not make this a big deal," she began. "Sherry is counting on us and we agreed to not only see the sights but to get to know some of the people."

"I've kept my feelings to myself all these years. I'm sure I can still do it."

She stared at him for a long moment, then put the car in gear and backed out of the parking space.

The sun had yet to rise, at five o'clock in the morning. McKenna drove to the restaurant and found one of the spaces allotted to employees. Parker was out of the car before she had even shut the engine off.

"It was always going to be a long trip," she muttered to herself.

Her door opened and Parker stood there, offering his hand. She contemplated taking it. If she refused his help, it would appear that she was still angry with him. The truth was, she didn't know how she felt.

McKenna put her hand in his and he helped angle her out of the car. However, he didn't step back, giving her the space to move any farther. He blocked her exit and she knew it was intentional.

Looking up at him, she tried to see what was in his eyes, but the darkness of the morning concealed it.

"I called the office and had them get another room for me. You can keep the one we've been sharing."

They hadn't discussed it, McKenna thought. All she could do was give a single nod.

"You'll be moving tonight?"

"I thought I'd run over after breakfast and move my things. If that's all right with you?"

She couldn't say yes or no. Her brain wasn't understanding what it was hearing. She wanted him to go, but then she didn't. He sounded as if he couldn't get far enough away from her.

She opened her hand, the one holding the car key. "While you're doing that, I'll stay here and help Sherry with the lunch setup."

He took the key, but his fingers never made contact with her hand. Did she want him to touch her? Was she disappointed that he hadn't? Yet he was standing so close. In the coolness of the pre-dawn, she could feel the heat emanating from him.

"Shall we go in?" she asked. McKenna noticed the dark windows of the restaurant. She knew Sherry was inside. Her car was parked in the lot next to where she'd put the Corvette.

"Only one more thing," he said.

"What's that?"

Parker was silent for so long, she lifted her eyes to look directly at him. Before she knew what he intended, his arm was around her waist and he'd dragged her the short distance that had separated them. With his other hand, he slipped it into her hair and brought her mouth to his. At first, McKenna thought she should push him back. It was logical to do that. But his mouth felt too good on hers. His arm around her was sure and strong. She'd forgotten what it felt like for a man to hold her. Emotions that she'd buried suddenly surfaced, like a strong gust of wind that sweeps around a corner taking you by surprise.

She went up on her toes, joining him in the kiss. It seemed to go on forever. But reality rushed in and she soon stepped out of his arms. How her own arms had gotten around him, she didn't know.

Parker stepped back also, moving out of her personal space. His stare was steady as she glanced up at him. "I'm not going to apologize," he said. "I'm not sorry."

McKenna couldn't speak. Her lip trembled from contact with his. Parker turned, but took her hand and headed toward the door.

"Come on," he said. "I can't leave you out here alone."

Was she sorry? McKenna asked herself. She didn't know. She never expected Parker to kiss her. She never expected to enjoy it. But she had. It had been a long while since Marshall's passing. She should be ready to date again, to find someone she could spend her life with.

But Parker?

He wasn't that man. Parker Fordum was the last man on earth that she could have any kind of romantic relationship with.

Sherry unlocked the door of the restaurant and she and Parker entered. McKenna was unsure if the tension and confusion between them would spill over, alerting Sherry or her customers once they arrived.

"Good morning." Sherry's smile was big and warm. She pulled the door closed and relocked it. When the first customer arrived at exactly 7:00 a.m., they went into busy mode and it continued until only a couple of tables were occupied.

They resumed their roles from the day before. Sherry looked after the grill and McKenna handled the floor. Parker worked both the floor and the cash register. Between breakfast and lunch, they cleaned and restocked supplies. When McKenna and Parker sat down to eat just before the lunch crowd was due to arrive, Parker intentionally sat next to McKenna.

She forced herself not to shift away from him. The tension was stronger than ever, but Parker ate quickly and left to return to the motel and move his things to another room.

"I didn't ask yesterday, but are you two married?" Sherry asked as they watched him go through the door.

McKenna shook her head.

"Engaged?"

"No." McKenna frowned. "Do we act like we're engaged?" She was unsure if what had happened in the parking lot had made it through the hostility that she felt.

"You did yesterday. Today I'm not so sure."

"What does that mean?" she asked after a long pause.

"You were friendlier yesterday," Sherry said. "Today, you're acting like polite strangers." She sat back in her seat. "I know we only met a day ago and I'm sorry if I'm speaking out of turn, but I've owned this place for twenty years and I've learned a lot about people."

McKenna leaned toward her. "So we act like we're together?"

"For him it's obvious. For you...well." She spread her hands, palms up. "You know how you feel."

As MCKENNA ENTERED her room later that day, she saw Parker's plastic keycard on the dresser. Its position on the edge exactly matched the ninety-degree angles of the furniture. It reminded her of the perfectly shelved books in a library, each one lined up neatly in rows. But the room was missing Parker. His presence was everywhere.

She looked at the two beds. It had been strange sleeping with a man in her room before. Now McKenna felt strange without Parker in the next bed or sitting in the chair at the table. She wanted to run her fingers along the surface, but turned away instead.

Parker's new room was at the other end of the building. She wondered if he intentionally took one that far from her or if it was the only one available. Restless, she paced back and forth from door to table. After working a full shift, she should be tired enough to sleep, but all day she'd been holding in her emotions. Now she was alone with only her thoughts and she couldn't stop them.

She and Parker had only shared a room for a couple of weeks. Finances and her own stubbornness forced them together. She felt lost without him. His computer wasn't on the desk. The absence of his constant typing or the sound of the videos he watched made the room so quiet it seemed loud. His toothbrush was gone from the bathroom. He wasn't there to talk to her. She missed that. She'd never thought about her loneliness after coming to terms with Marshall's death. She knew she'd replaced Marshall with work. But she didn't have that here.

Then there was Sherry's comment which had played like a chant in her mind all day. *You know how you feel*, Sherry had said. But that was the problem. McKenna didn't know how she felt. She was confused. She couldn't have feelings for the man who hadn't saved her husband.

McKenna paced over the same floor that Parker had walked the night before. Then she remembered that they were supposed to discuss their kiss. Mainly it was his comment about keeping his hands off her. They were past that now. He'd had his hands on her and she hadn't stopped it, or regretted it.

How were they going to act with each other away from the diner? She needed to get that straight, especially in light of what Sherry had observed. McKenna knew his room number. And she couldn't put it off until morning. For them, morning came in the middle of the night. She considered whether she should go knock on his door and initiate the conversation. They needed to talk. It didn't appear that he was going to come to her. He'd said all that needed to be said this morning when his mouth was on hers.

Suddenly her lips tingled. McKenna put her hand to them, recalling the emotions that flooded into her as he held her. Sitting down, she took a deep breath and steadied herself. Then she got up and walked the distance to Parker's room. She'd raised her hand to knock, but Parker opened the door. They stared at each other for a second, their eyes connecting in unexpected surprise.

"We have to talk," they both said in unison.

McKenna didn't wait for an invitation. She breezed past him and stopped in the center of the room. Parker closed the door and turned to face her.

Looking around, she said, "This is a small room. Is it the only one they had available?"

"It was the cheapest one they had available. We're still on a budget," he reminded McKenna.

He took a step toward her. McKenna stepped back but then wished she hadn't.

Parker saw her reaction. "I'm not going to kiss you again," he said.

Her ears flared hot and color had to have darkened her face. She didn't know if that made her glad or sad. Since last night, her emotions had swung manically up and down.

"We've got a long way to go to get to California. We can't tiptoe around each other and act like we've done something wrong." She was nervous. Parker's expression was unreadable. At least he didn't say anything to make her feel even more uncomfortable.

"ARE YOU APOLOGIZING?"

"What?" McKenna shook her head once. "What would I have to apologize for?"

"For responding to my kiss."

McKenna gasped. She couldn't deny it, although those words were on the tip of her tongue. She had responded. In fact, if he hadn't pushed her away, their mouths might still be locked together.

"You said you weren't sorry."

"But you didn't." He took another step toward her.

McKenna retaliated by stepping back.

"Are you going to do that every time I come near you?"

"Only if I don't know what you intend to do." She wanted to leave the room, but Parker, as big as Paul Bunyan, loomed between her and the door.

"McKenna, I would never come toward you with anything but kind intent. You're as safe with me as you would be with…your husband."

"I notice you avoid mentioning Marshall's name," McKenna said. She stared directly at Parker.

He looked at her levelly, not blinking and not allowing any expression to appear in his eyes.

"Why do you say that?"

"Because every time I bring him up, you turn your head. Or you change the subject."

He didn't speak for a while, but he didn't drop his gaze, either. "I thought it might be a touchy subject with you."

"Me? Why?"

"Because you blame me for his death."

"I do, but—"

"Don't deny it." He raised a hand to stop

her comment. "I know you do and you know you do. So there's no point in lying."

"I wasn't going to lie."

"It was an accident," Parker said softly.

"I know," she said. But she didn't really understand. Marshall knew his condition and so did Parker. If Parker was the friend he was supposed to be, he should never have let Marshall make that final run.

"Marshall was a grown man, McKenna."

McKenna straightened her shoulders as if shrugging off something heavy, but she knew she wasn't.

"We're not here to discuss Marshall," she said.

"No, we never discuss Marshall. You've created a world where only you and he exist."

McKenna stepped back as if he'd hit her. "I have not."

"If that's true, then why are we on this trip?"

She threw her hands up. "I explained that."

"You did, but did you tell the truth?"

"Are you accusing me of lying again?

"Not intentionally. I believe you're not being honest with yourself."

McKenna was totally lost now. "I have no idea what you're talking about."

"You said this trip was your and Marshall's idea." This time he used Marshall's name. "That it was something the two of you always wanted to do."

"It was," she confirmed.

"It wasn't."

Parker winced. The tension between them had never been so thick.

"Marshall told me years ago about his wish to drive Route 66." His voice was softer now, calm like it usually was. "He obviously told you about it and somewhere, somehow you came to believe it was a common goal, but it wasn't. Marshall was the one with the replica of the car in his office. You built your car exactly like the one that sat on his credenza. But in truth, the Corvette used in the television series was blue, not red."

He was right. It had been Marshall's dream. They'd talked about it often and then after his death she'd started building the car. The more she worked on it, the more it became something *she* wanted. And now they—or rather, she and Parker—were on the road, halfway to California and this wasn't even her dream.

"McKenna?" Parker broke into her thoughts.

"You're right, Parker. I'd forgotten. I suppose we should turn around and head back to Chicago."

"I didn't say that. Please don't put words in my mouth."

Anger flared inside McKenna. "Why did you come, Parker? If you knew this was all a lie in my mind, why are you here? You can't want to go on. You never did. Why would you, now that I've acknowledged the truth? I guess we should just call it a day and return home."

"I said I wasn't going to kiss you. And I'm not. But you need to be kissed, thoroughly."

"Not by you. Which proves you don't know everything, Parker."

McKenna lobbed the words at him, but wondered if he could tell how her chest heaved up and down as she drew breath. Or if he shared her thought that they were standing too close to one another, that more distance would be better.

"I only want to say that this has become something you want to do, McKenna, and we've agreed to see it through to the end. I have no problem keeping my end of the deal. And I've never had the idea that you wanted to end it. But things have changed. We can't pretend they haven't."

"No, we can't."

"Do you want to complete the trip?"

"I like what we're doing. I enjoyed helping Joanna and I like Sherry, although I don't know her well."

"And I like taking jobs I usually wouldn't think of doing. I've never had to do that. Even though you forced me into it, I'm glad to be here."

McKenna watched the way he looked at her. She knew it would not be the same from now on. The two of them had crossed a threshold. She wouldn't allow it to go any further, but they couldn't pretend that it hadn't happened.

"We go on," she said.

CHAPTER EIGHT

BOTH MCKENNA AND PARKER stepped out of their rooms at the same time. McKenna looked down the long colonnade. Parker lifted his hand and waved. McKenna let a breath out. She was glad they were still friends, she thought. She didn't like arguing with him.

She sure did like kissing him; it hadn't been all one-sided. She had responded to it, to him. But she couldn't let it happen again. They met at the car with a smile.

"I'll drive," he said and McKenna immediately handed him the key.

"Sleep well?" he asked.

"I did," she answered honestly. "Have to admit, I'm used to you being in the room. It felt a bit weird without you. But I settled down and didn't wake up until the clock alarm went off. How about you?"

"I missed you, too," he said.

An economy of words, McKenna noticed. They drove the rest of the way in silence and went right to work. As usual the restaurant was busy. They barely had time for anything until after lunch.

While Parker cleaned the grill and Sherry cleared the last of the patrons' dishes away, McKenna returned from the pantry with an idea.

"Sherry, do you mind if I make something to add to the menu tonight?" McKenna asked.

"You cook, too?" Sherry questioned, adding the dishes to the nearly full dishwasher.

"I'm not a gourmet, but for good ole plain food I can hold my own."

"What have you got in mind?" She flipped the switch on the machine and the sound of water immediately filled the space.

Sherry headed back to the dining room. McKenna followed.

"Corn pudding and banana bread," she said. "We can pair the corn pudding with one of the meats, say the lamb chops, and call it a special. The customer will get the banana bread as a dessert."

"It sounds good, but have you ever cooked for a hundred people?"

"I've cooked for twenty on Thanksgiving, and I know how to multiply a recipe. Some recipes can only be done in batches, but these are not that kind. It'll work. And we can sell the dinner at a special price."

"I'm game. Do we have all the ingredients you need?"

"I checked. We have everything, including some overripe bananas."

"I was going to throw those out."

"Now we have a use for them."

"If this goes well, you should get credit for it."

"It's a family recipe. I expect it to go well, but if it doesn't, I'll take the heat."

"If it doesn't go well, we'll just chalk it up to experience," Sherry said. "I've had my share of disasters." She paused and adjusted her apron. "Are you going to need help?"

"I know you have to get the other dishes ready. Parker will help me." She wasn't completely sure how he'd feel about her having volunteered him. "And we'll fill in to help where you need us. Prep time is short, especially with the equipment you have. But we'll manage." McKenna wanted to assure Parker that things between them were back on solid footing. Working together would let him know she held no hard feelings from their argument yesterday.

"Did I hear my name?" Parker said from the kitchen doorway.

"You and I are going to make something special for the dinner crowd," McKenna told him.

"You'll need to make extra. Tonight is Friday and we always get truckers from the highway popping in for a meal," Sherry said.

Within minutes McKenna had given Parker instructions on what to do to make the bread. He took direction well and went to work like a pro. McKenna started on the corn pudding. Each of them used a section of the large center counter. Sherry kept looking over at what the two of them were doing. McKenna wondered if Sherry was nervous and if she was wasting the woman's costly inventory.

"Where'd you learn to cook, Parker?" Sherry asked. "You took to that grill yesterday as if you'd been at it for years and now this, with almost no instruction. McKenna hasn't had to say another word."

"I learned out of necessity," he said. "As a kid, I hung around the kitchen a lot. Then in college I was a short-order cook at a pancake house."

"Really?" McKenna was shocked.

He smiled. "Another thing you didn't know about me." He winked at her. "I paid for a lot of my misspent youth on the salary of a cook."

"Did you think of going into the business, becoming a chef?" Sherry asked.

Parker shook his head. "Don't get me wrong, I love a good home-cooked meal. But I don't want cooking to comprise my entire day, every day."

"So, what comprises most of your day?" Sherry asked.

Parker peeled and broke bananas, adding them to the industrial-size mixing bowl. "I teach economics at a university."

"Ah, so that's why you took to the cash register like it was an extension of your hands."

"Where are the loaf pans?" he asked.

"Bottom shelf, over there."

Sherry indicated a stainless steel cabinet in the corner. Parker bent down and opened the double doors. Reaching inside, he found dozens of pans.

"What does economics do for you that cooking doesn't?" McKenna joined in.

Parker stood up and stared through the kitchen toward the dining room windows. "Food doesn't light up."

"Light up?" Sherry stopped seasoning the lamb chops that would go with the corn pudding and both women stared at the only man in the room.

He turned to them. "You both know what I'm talking about. It's when the lightbulb goes on. When one of my students finally understands a concept that has eluded him or her, it's like seeing a light turn on. One day all the pieces fall into place and you suddenly understand a concept or an equation and then wonder why you ever thought it was so difficult. Remember when you learned your times tables? At first it was just memorize it, but later you saw the logic of how to figure it out."

Both women smiled. "For me it was long division," Sherry said.

Parker moved back to his work station and turned off the mixer. The whine of the motor wound down, leaving the kitchen with only the hum of the restaurant-size refrigerator.

"It happens spontaneously," he went on. "The lightbulb flashes and words tumble out of their mouths. When I see it, when I hear it, I know I've reached into the mind of someone and opened a door. It's exhilarating. You can't get that from cooking."

"Okay," McKenna said, thinking of a baker designing a cake and practicing getting all the roses in icing to look alike. She watched him complete the recipe she'd given him and begin to pour the batter into the loaf pans.

"Obviously, there's a lot more to you, Parker, than meets the eye," Sherry commented. "When I hired you two, I was desperate, but you're turning out to be a godsend."

"What about you, Sherry?" McKenna asked. "How'd you become a restaurant owner?"

"Oh, that's a long story."

"We've got time before the dinner crowd arrives." Parker put the first batch of banana bread in the oven. Then he opened the refrigerator, got three bottles of water and handed them out. Sherry had explained the importance of remaining hydrated while they worked.

"Do you think this will be too much?" He'd found thirty loaf pans and filled them with batter. Half of them were in the oven.

"They freeze well, if they aren't all used tonight," McKenna jumped in.

"Thirty should be enough to begin with," Sherry agreed. "If these new recipes really take off, you know I'm going to be up the creek when you two leave."

"I'll give you the recipes," McKenna said. "You can bake the bread at night and stockpile it and the pudding in the freezer."

Parker started cleaning the equipment he'd used.

"I was a divorced mother of two girls, ages seven and nine," Sherry told them. "My husband left me and took everything we had. The bank foreclosed on the house and the state was threatening to take my kids."

"Oh, no." McKenna reacted with a jolt.

Sherry gave her a reassuring smile. "It worked out," she assured McKenna before going on with the story. "I had an aunt who lived here in a small house. She was ailing and needed someone to care for her. I agreed to do it so we'd have someplace to live, but she wasn't rich, so we had to have an income."

Sherry stared at her hands holding the bottle of water. McKenna knew she was looking into the past.

"I started working the lunch shift and preparing food for the dinner menu. I did it in my aunt's kitchen and brought it over in time for the rush hour. My aunt died and left us the house. I worked full time after that and eventually the owner wanted to retire. He offered to sell the restaurant to me. I could barely afford shoes for my girls, so I couldn't pay for it. But he made me a deal where he held the mortgage. I never missed a payment. When he died three years later, his will cancelled the debt, leaving me the business free and clear. I've maintained it ever since."

"You used economics in doing that," Parker said, replacing the bowl on the mixer. "And you do it every day when determining what supplies you need and how much food to get ready for each meal to keep waste at a minimum."

Sherry raised her arms and shouted, "I'm an economist. Who knew?"

They all laughed.

McKenna's corn pudding went in the oven as the first batch of bread came out. An hour later everything was ready.

The bell over the door jingled as the first diner appeared.

"Sherry, I don't know what you got going back there, but I'll take two helpings," someone shouted.

Sherry grinned. "That's Mike. Drives an 18-wheeler from St. Louis to Phoenix. Always drops in for a meal. I think your menu item is going to be a hit." Sherry slipped out of the kitchen to take Mike's order.

McKenna turned to Parker. "Since you're

good at writing on blackboards, why don't you list the specials for tonight?"

INSTEAD OF BEING tired after the long day, McKenna was exhilarated. Parker was like a giant puzzle to her. As their trip had progressed, he'd become more and more enigmatic, but between last night and today, she'd learned a lot about him and felt as if she understood him better. And she liked him better, too.

After the last dinner guest left and the cleaning was completed, Sherry brought decaf coffee to one of the tables and the three of them sat down for a few moments of calm. The night had been hectic. The diner had quickly filled with patrons; three times before closing there must have been a turnover of customers. McKenna had needed help on the floor. Parker pitched in and did what he could. McKenna hadn't counted her tips, but she was sure tonight was a career high for her in the restaurant trade.

"Sorry, there's no banana bread to go with the coffee," Sherry said.

"I should have made more. We'll do it

for tomorrow." Parker looked at McKenna as he said it.

She nodded.

"Where'd you say that recipe came from?" Sherry asked.

"It's been in my family for a long time. My mother gave it to me in one of her cookbooks," McKenna told her. "I tried it one night when I was in high school and it turned out well. I make it every year, usually around Christmastime. But tonight I thought it might be good for business."

"You were right there." Sherry confirmed. "People bought entire loaves to take with them. And who thought they'd pay that much for one loaf of bread?"

They both looked at Parker.

"Our economist," McKenna said.

"It was worth it," Parker added. "First it tasted fantastic and it was a perfect illustration of the law of supply and demand."

"We had demand," Sherry said. "We even took orders."

McKenna sipped her coffee.

"The corn pudding was a hit, too," Sherry

went on. "I've had it before, but it never tasted like yours."

"We can thank my grandmother." McKenna bowed her head.

"You know what? You should consider selling other items," Parker suggested, still in his capacity as an economist.

"What do you mean?" Sherry asked.

"Offering baked goods, desserts, breads that people can order. Maybe adding catering to your services."

"Hold on, professor," Sherry said, her hand telling him to back off. "I'm having serious personnel problems. No way could I add baked goods for order and catering. When would I sleep?"

"And I think you should put up a billboard on the highway, enticing people to dine here." Parker continued as if Sherry hadn't said anything. "The food is good and they get a little treat with the special. Who knows, in time you could have more than one restaurant."

"Does he often go on like this?" Sherry directed her question to McKenna.

"He hasn't until now. I guess business is one of his hot buttons."

Parker's eyes flashed at McKenna and she wanted to pull the words back as soon as they were out. She turned back to Sherry.

"It's not a bad idea he's got," McKenna told her. "Eventually, you could set up a bakery section." McKenna scanned the floor plan. "You could even have a revolving stand by the door so people see the baked goods when they come in. If you knocked out that wall." She indicated the end of the dining room. "You could build a room and put the display cases there."

Parker nodded as if the decision had already been made.

"During holidays, proms, birthdays, parties, you could supply the baked goods. Is there already a bakery in town?" Parker asked.

Sherry shook her head, looking as if the suggestions were one step too far. "You know you two could be dangerous."

"Yeah, but wouldn't it be fun?" McKenna said.

RETURNING TO THE motel after closing the restaurant was more comfortable between them than it had been when they'd left it early this morning, Parker thought. McKenna's idea of making recipes for the daily special helped. He might be an economist, but he didn't miss her subtle intentions. She was breaking the ice between them. At least, she was melting the last pieces of it by working with him and giving him credit for the most talked about meal the restaurant had had in years.

He pulled the car into a parking space right outside her room and they got out. As they stepped onto the walkway, his room seemed miles from hers.

"I guess this is good night," McKenna said. She'd made no attempt to find her key or to enter her room.

"It was a good day," Parker said.

"I liked your ideas about expanding the restaurant. It reminded me of how the auto business expanded."

"Sherry would take in a lot, but I understand her reluctance. She's only one person."

"More economic facts?" McKenna smiled.

"I can't help it. It's how my mind works."

"Don't apologize. I'm getting used to how your mind works."

He laughed. "That's great, because I have no idea how yours works."

McKenna smiled as if his comment was a compliment. "It works much like yours. We all have a little economist in us."

"And a little adventurer."

He watched the smile spread across her face. She was an adventurer, traversing her own jungle in pursuit of a dream. After a moment, the silence stretched. "I guess this is good night," Parker said.

He watched as she turned to her door. He also moved toward the door and so they collided with each other. He caught her at the waist and steadied her. She looked up at him. Despite the darkness, the light above the door shone clearly into her eyes. He saw concern mixed with something unreadable, but it was soft and warm.

No doubt she thought he'd forgotten that they no longer shared the same space. His room was the width of the building away from hers.

"I thought I'd check your room before leaving," Parker said.

McKenna moved back. She opened her

purse and retrieved the plastic keycard. Parker took it and preceded her into the room. He was already familiar with it.

Parker checked the closet and bathroom. His clothes were obviously gone and his toothbrush no longer lay on the glass shelf.

"Everything looks all right," he said, his smile tight.

"Thank you."

He nodded. Taking a step to the door, he noticed the desk where his computer often sat. The space was clear.

"I'll be going. See you in the morning."

"Good night."

Parker left without a backward glance. He wanted to look back, but if she had the same softness to her eyes he'd seen before they'd come in the room, he'd cross the imaginary line they both knew existed.

Unlocking his room, he went inside the unfamiliar space.

He switched the television on for some noise. They'd eaten dinner at the restaurant with Sherry, so Parker wasn't hungry. But he felt as if he'd left part of himself back outside McKenna's door.

SOMETHING OR SOMEONE was banging something together. McKenna's groggy mind tried to shut out the sound.

"McKenna?"

Someone called to her. It was Parker. The recognition had her eyes wide open and she sat up in bed as if propelled. Something had happened. Throwing the covers aside, she rushed to the door and opened it.

"What's wrong?" she asked.

"Aren't you up yet?" Parker said by way of an answer.

"What time is it?" McKenna pushed her hand through her hair as she turned and looked at the huge numbers on the digital clock. "I overslept," she said, stating the obvious. "Come in. I'll be dressed in no time."

She didn't wait for him to come fully in the room. She hurried into the bathroom, brushed her teeth, pushed a hairband onto her head to hold the strands back and added just lipstick to her face.

Coming out, she grabbed a pair of pants and a T-shirt from the drawer. Parker sat at the table. His computer lay on the surface in front of him. His eyes followed her from place to place. Quickly she dressed in the bathroom and came out.

"Ready," she said.

Parker got up. "You're the only woman I know who can get ready in ten minutes and look sensational."

"Is that a compliment?"

"Most certainly."

"Thank you, but we have to go." McKenna didn't have time to deal with kind sentiments from Parker. He made her nervous at times, especially when he acted nice and got on subjects she'd rather not discuss.

"What's on the menu today?" Parker asked as he drove.

"I'm not sure. We didn't really do a lot of dishes that weren't just plain food."

"That's what Sherry sells," Parker reminded her. "What about a dessert?"

"I'm terrible at those. I can do the breads, but cakes, cookies, not my thing." She shook her head. "I'll check Sherry's cookbooks and see what's there that's simple, and I can experiment with it."

"So far you've been on the money. And Sherry appreciates it."

"With all the new business coming in, she can afford to hire a cook."

"Those new customers might only be here because of your recipes," Parker said.

McKenna heard the compliment that was couched in his comment. "I'm sure she or her daughter will be able to duplicate the recipes. And her daughter may have specialties of her own. I think it was just a matter of showing Sherry that giving something different now and then would bring people back time and again."

"Creating demand," Parker said.

"By the time we get to the west coast, I'll be well versed in economics."

"And I'll have added restaurateur to my list of expertise."

At the diner the day began as it usually did. Sherry asked if McKenna had anything she wanted to add to the menu. She'd replied that she did and added strawberry crepes and cherry blintzes to the breakfast items.

And she'd convinced Sherry to try a theme night. All Italian dishes once a week made ordering easier, and who would think so many people would show up for roast beef and Yorkshire pudding, not to mention breakfast scones with clotted cream? Customers filled the parking lot the minute the place opened. Sherry's was busy from morning to night.

"You know, I said you two were a godsend when you picked up those first plates and started working for me," Sherry said as Parker and McKenna began their final week in her restaurant.

McKenna nodded, glancing at Parker. Both waited for her to go on.

"Are you sure you don't want to stay on? I've never had so much business. And I know it's due to your recipes and Parker's having taken over the cooking. I'd be willing to find you a place to live and you could live here permanently."

Both of them started to say something, but Sherry stopped them.

"I was only kidding about the permanent thing, unless you'd really consider it."

"Our home is in Chicago," Parker replied.

"I've given you the recipes and you can make the dishes," McKenna told her. "They're not hard. You've seen us do it. And they don't have to be *these* dishes. You can make what you want. Just change things up once in a while."

"Your daughter is due soon," Parker said. "She is still coming?"

"I spoke with her yesterday. She's cleared up some problems and she'll be here tomorrow."

"That's wonderful." McKenna smiled.

"Are you anxious to be on your way?" Sherry asked. "I guess you stayed here longer than you do in most places."

"We're not on a tight schedule," Parker commented.

McKenna glanced at Parker. Not long ago she thought he'd want to get the trip over as quickly as possible. But somewhere they'd rounded a bend and were all the better for it. A burst of emotion filled her heart.

CHAPTER NINE

SAYING GOODBYE WAS never easy for Mc-
Kenna. With Sherry it was especially hard.
Her daughter, Crystal, arrived as scheduled.
She was just as delightful as her mother and
McKenna could see the special relationship
they shared. For a moment she missed her
own mother, both parents actually. They
died young. McKenna was a semester away
from college graduation when they were involved in a car accident on a bridge near
their home. If it hadn't been for Marshall,
she couldn't imagine how she would have
gotten through the loss.

Crystal was awed by the number of customers seated or waiting to be seated as
Parker and McKenna's final days wound
down. They spent part of the week explaining to her what had been going on. The other
part was Crystal and McKenna working the

floor and Parker and Sherry in the kitchen keeping up with orders. McKenna was glad to see Sherry's daughter had ideas of her own and she'd brought her favorite cookbook. During the three days before they said goodbye, they made several dishes, which she chose. Those were as much a hit with the customers as the others had been.

"Things are going to be fine after we're gone," Parker commented the night before they left.

As Sherry hugged her goodbye and asked her to keep in touch, she told her she felt confident and more excited about the restaurant than she had in years. McKenna trembled inside as emotional feelings lodged in her throat and misty tears threatened to take her voice away. She would miss Sherry and Crystal, but she was taking happy memories with her.

McKenna took a satisfying breath and settled in for the ride. It wasn't unusual to drive Route 66 and not pass another car for miles. Then suddenly the roadway would be littered with them, everybody driving ten miles an hour when there was nothing to see. McKenna had experienced both scenarios as they traveled this much-loved although sometimes rocky road. The traffic eventually thinned, and soon her Corvette was back to being the only car on the road.

"What are you watching?" she asked Parker. He wore earbuds and had his computer propped on his knees, so he might not have heard her. Glancing at the screen, McKenna could barely see anything other than a movie in black and white.

"An old rerun," he answered.

"Of what?"

"Route 66."

McKenna leaned over and glanced at the screen for the three seconds it was safe. Then her eyes were back on the road.

He cleared his throat. "The stories are very interesting."

"I have the entire collection back at home." She didn't tell him she knew the episodes by heart. All she needed to see was the opening sequence and she could tell him the entire plotline.

"In this one, they're in Boston seeing the sights."

McKenna smiled. "To Walk with the Serpent."

"What, you have them memorized?" He glanced at her.

She grinned, but kept her attention on the road in front of her.

"You do have them memorized."

"Most of them. In that one they meet a man named John Westerbrook."

Parker pulled the earbuds free. The expression on his face told her he was both surprised and in awe of her knowledge.

"Do you want me to go on?" she asked.

"I'll finish watching it later. I am amazed that you have all that in your head."

"What, did you only think I knew about engines, axels and the dynamics of road travel?"

"Not exactly. I didn't know that you could cook, that you have a weird sense of humor, that you're also the most stubborn woman I've ever met and that you are so compassionate that a lost teenager could keep you awake at night."

Another wave of emotion went through her. There was easy approval in his voice and it made her feel good that he liked what she'd done, how she'd felt.

"It's what interests me, although I disagree with you about the stubborn part. But what about you? You told me you once wanted to play in a band. Other than that I know very little about you. You're a professor of economics. You've been married and divorced. And you're very protective of me." She kept her eyes down when she said that, but chanced a look at him.

Parker glanced at her, but his expression told her nothing. "I wouldn't want you hurt during the trip of a lifetime."

"Thank you." She wondered if that was all there was to his comment. Inside, she suddenly felt hollow. She remembered his arms around her as he pulled her away from the door the night of the robbery. Each time after that, he'd been very aware of their surroundings. Even the night in the motel, when they returned to separate rooms, he'd checked hers to make sure it was safe for her to enter.

"I'm sure you have a wealth of topics that

occupy your attention and have nothing to do with being a professor of economics."

He grinned at her. McKenna liked that way he smiled. His mouth wasn't totally straight, but it wasn't a lopsided grin, either.

"So what else do you like to do? And by the way, I'm not the only stubborn one in this car."

"We'll just call it being persistent." He paused a moment. "I like camping. You know I enjoy skiing."

"Can you ice-skate, too?"

"Who grows up in Chicago and doesn't ice-skate? It's practically a law. We used to go to this park every day in the winter."

"We?"

"Gerald and Ellie, my brother and sister. Of course, it helped that there were girls there." He winked at her and they both smiled. "We'd pull our skates on. Gerald was the better skater than I was, but if you ever meet him I'll deny I told you that."

McKenna was enjoying Parker more and more. She felt he rarely opened up to anyone and she was glad he'd chosen to tell her such personal details.

"We'd show off our skills to get the girls to notice us."

"And did they?"

He nodded. "Ellie is in China because of one of the guys she met on the ice. Although it was years later that they ran into each other and got together. He was the recruiter when she only had an engineering degree and wanted to make her mark on the world."

"What's she doing in China?"

"Building a dam. And teaching English to Chinese children." He laughed. "I never dreamed that my little sister would end up changing the world."

We all change the world, McKenna thought. *Even if it's only a small square of earth, it changes us*. She was thinking of Joanna and Sherry. Had their lives been altered by coming into contact with her and Parker? And where would the two of them go, now that their lives had been hopefully enriched by someone else?

"You know what I've always wanted to do?"

McKenna brought her attention back to Parker. "What?"

Parker looked up at the sky. "Skydiving."

She looked up, too. "That's a great idea. Why don't you do it?"

"McKenna, I don't think they have skydiving along Route 66."

"You never know. The route goes south of Phoenix. We could detour for a few days and go there."

"Why Phoenix?"

"They have the best airspace for ballooning."

Parker frowned. "This is one of those times when I have no idea how your mind works."

"Sorry," she said. "My thoughts were running ahead of my mouth. We can arrange it so we're in Phoenix for the balloon show in July. It's huge and something I've always wanted to see."

"See, not do?"

"All right, do. The point is, we can see the balloon show and you can go skydiving."

He hesitated. "I'll think about it."

"Think about it," she repeated. "Why not do it? Come on."

"Because I'm no longer that ten-year-old kid zooming around the ice or…"

McKenna shifted in her seat. "Let me ask you a question. What do you want written on your tombstone?"

"What? Are you saying skydiving will kill me and you're preparing for my death?"

"Not at all. Do you want it to read, *Things I Wish I'd Done*?"

"You know, you're really good at guilting people."

"I won't force you. I'm merely saying think about getting out of your comfort zone and doing something you want to do."

"And if I fall on my face, you'll be there to catch me?"

"I'll give it an honest try," McKenna said. "After all, I owe you."

"Owe me?"

"You caught me when I was about to run into a dangerous situation."

Parker thought about that. McKenna saw his expression change when he remembered keeping her from sprinting into her room the night of the theft.

"When we get to Arizona, we can check

into the particulars. I'm sure I can't just strap on a parachute and jump out of a plane."

"Sounds like fun," she said.

"I take it skydiving is not on your bucket list."

"It's not."

"What about ballooning?"

"Nope." She shook her head. "But if you need a partner in the sky, I'll try it."

"Our funds are still in question. Skydiving is expensive. For two it'd be twice as expensive."

"As an economist you're not opposed to spending money, are you?"

"Money makes the world turn round," he stated, matter of factly.

"So, it's money. I always thought it was love that turned the world round."

"CATOOSA, FIFTY MILES." Parker read the sign-post as they passed it on a lonely strip of Oklahoma blacktop that was cracked and spit shards of gravel against the car's un-blemished paint job. Despite the sign, the landscape didn't change. It was flat, sporting fields colored a goldish-brown.

"We're going to see the blue whale, right?" Parker asked.

"You're really getting into this, aren't you?"

"It's that tombstone comment that has me wanting to be Bob Cratchit and not Ebenezer Scrooge."

McKenna laughed. "You would never be Scrooge."

"Does that mean you've changed your opinion of me?"

McKenna checked her rearview mirror. "I have." Her voice was so low, she wasn't sure Parker would hear her. She'd changed her mind on a lot of things related to Parker. He was much more than she'd given him credit for. He wasn't the trapped-in-the-box person she'd accused him of being. He was concerned for her and for other people. He was the first to see that Joanna needed help. And when they arrived at Sherry's restaurant, he didn't question McKenna about helping out.

The only blemish she could see was him leaving the room they shared. McKenna knew their finances were precarious. That had not changed, even though Sherry had given them much more than necessary as payment for bringing in customers and giving her a hand when she was desperate. Yet the bottom line was that she missed his presence, sharing his space.

"Where are you, McKenna? You look as if you're trying to solve a hard problem."

"I was just thinking."

"About what?" Parker asked.

"You've told me some things about you, but you never mention your marriage or your ex-wife."

She watched Parker's shoulders drop as if he was struggling under a huge weight.

"What happened?"

He sighed heavily and took a long time before he spoke. McKenna was about to apologize for asking when he began to talk.

"We were only married for a short time," he said. "A little longer than a year. Only fifteen months, actually."

That was a short time. She and Marshall were married for almost six years before he died. Had it not been for Marshall's condition and that final trip down the mountain, the two would still be husband and wife.

"I take it the split wasn't amicable."

"No, it was."

She looked at him, waiting for an explanation, but believing she'd stepped across bounds that should not be breached.

"We both got married for the wrong reasons. She was defying her parents."

"They didn't approve of you?"

"That wasn't it. They liked me well enough. I wasn't their choice for a son-in-law, but they never spoke meanly or made me feel as if I wasn't welcome in their family. She just wasn't ready for marriage, not to me or to the man her parents favored. We were both too young, too immature. We didn't understand what love was, what marriage meant."

"You weren't in love with her?"

He winced. "She wasn't in love with me, either. It didn't take us long to discover the truth."

"Truth?" McKenna frowned.

"I was in love, but with someone else. It became obvious, and we decided the best thing to do was to dissolve our marriage."

How mature, McKenna thought, but kept

the words to herself. This was more like the Parker she knew. He'd calculate that it was time to end the marriage and he and his bride would fill in all the necessary paperwork and walk away, as simply as if they'd erased a part of their lives. Still, she was sorry for him. He loved someone else. That must be hard if the feelings weren't reciprocated. She wanted to ask who, and why he didn't marry the woman he was in love with, but thought that was a subject even she couldn't broach. Parker deserved his secrets.

"I'm sorry it didn't work out," she said, feeling the platitude was useless.

"Don't be. We recognized our mistake before things got out of hand."

"You mean children?"

He nodded.

"What happened to her? Did she go back and marry the man her parents chose?"

"She's still unmarried. The last I heard, she'd moved to Seattle and opened a bed-and-breakfast." He grunted more than laughed, although there was a smile on his face. "She was from St. Louis. I suppose moving was her last act of defiance against her parents."

"You admire her."

"I do," he said. "She's intelligent, able to admit her mistakes, unafraid to strike out on her own and try something new. She's a strong woman, deserving of my respect and admiration." He glanced at McKenna. "She's a lot like you."

"But you told me I was crazy for going on a trip like this. That I was stubborn and foolish."

"I said you were crazy for trying to go it alone."

"I stand corrected," McKenna said. Then she asked. "Did you ever see her after the divorce?"

"Once. We ran into each other in Minneapolis at the Mall of America, of all places." Again he grunted the laugh. "I was there for a conference and discovered cologne spilled on my dress shirt. The stain wouldn't come out, so I rushed to get another shirt. She was visiting a friend. We had a nice long lunch together and that was the last time we spoke."

McKenna pictured it in her mind. She could see him heading in one direction and a faceless woman in the other. The two would briefly turn and wave goodbye. Then each would be swallowed by the crowd.

"I suppose you and Marshall never had any doubts about your marriage?"

She looked at him straight on. "All marriages have periods when things are not ideal, but no, I never doubted I loved him. And I never doubted he loved me."

Parker lapsed into silence at that. McKenna continued to drive, but she couldn't help wondering who the woman was that Parker had been in love with when he'd married someone else.

"Why haven't you ever married again?"

"Haven't found the right woman."

It was the old cliché, McKenna thought, however, it didn't sound like a cliché when Parker said it.

"You haven't had any serious relationships since her?"

"I didn't say that. I just never found anyone I wanted to see from across the breakfast table for the rest of my life."

"Hopefully, you'll find someone you will want to spend your life with."

"I guess being in love makes life worth-while," Parker said.

"It sounds silly, but it does."

"Maybe the same will happen to you."

McKenna instantly dismissed the notion. "I doubt it."

"Why? You're a young woman, beauti-ful, independent. There must be a thousand guys vying for your hand. You're not going to hide away for the rest of your life, are you? Marshall wouldn't want that."

Speaking of platitudes, that sounded like one, and McKenna had heard it more than once from her friends. "No," she agreed. "Marshall wouldn't have wanted that. But I'm not in the market for a man." She wanted to say there was plenty of time, but Marshall's death showed her how quickly life could end.

Forty miles to Catoosa. McKenna noted the signpost as they passed it. They were going to spend the night there. There was a huge tourist display and they'd agreed to visit it.

"What's her name?" McKenna went back to the earlier part of their conversation.

"Whose name?"

"Your ex-wife."

"Loretta Bellamy."

"Bellamy, that sounds familiar," she murmured, frowning, trying to remember where she'd heard it before.

"It should," he said softly.

"Why?"

"When we met, she was seeing someone else."

"You told me that," she reminded him.

"Don't you recall who she was seeing?"

McKenna tried to remember. She tried to see the face of the woman Parker was being so obscure about.

"College. She was in college with us. I was several years behind you," she said. Then the lightbulb went off. "She was Marshall's girlfriend."

"She was attracted to him. Not the other way around."

"He never told me that." McKenna was sure of it.

"It probably never occurred to him. Once you came on the scene, he was blind to every other woman."

Something in Parker's tone had her looking at him. He didn't seem to be talking about Marshall. His voice was quieter than she was used to hearing it. His tone was caressing and it did something to her that wasn't at all unpleasant.

"So, in a way, you were both on the rebound."

"She was."

"Not you?"

"You have to have been in a relationship to rebound from someone. You can't do it all by yourself."

So it was unrequited love, she concluded, feeling sorry for Parker. But she couldn't help wondering who the woman was that could crack Parker's shell.

"Watch out," Parker shouted.

McKenna saw the deer too late. She swerved the car trying to get out of its path. The deer raced across the road in front of her. She swerved back to the correct lane, but another deer came at her, following the first. Biting down on her lip, she knew she was going to hit it. There was nothing she could do to stop the collision.

Unconsciously, her arm came out and crossed Parker's chest, pressing him back in the seat, instinctively protecting him. Jerking the steering wheel left at the very last second, she managed to avoid a direct hit. The car clipped the deer's legs. It faltered, fell on the pavement, but got up and ran on. The roadway was broken and the car bumped and jumped as it hit potholes. She heard the squeal of tires and smelled burning rubber as she tried to maintain control of the small vehicle. It ran over the dirt shoulder and into a field. Brush sounds replaced the skidding as the car mowed over long grass.

Thirty yards off the road and five feet from a tree, the car came to a stop. Momentum forced her forward, but the seat belt kept her in the car, wrenched her backward, her head making a hard impact on the nonstandard head rest. Her hand was still protecting Parker.

The engine hissed and smoke bellowed from under the hood. McKenna took a deep breath and studied Parker. Releasing the seat belt, she opened her door and fell out of the car. She tried to get to her feet but her legs felt like rubber. She took in great mouthfuls of air, forcing it into her lungs as she tried to stand again.

Strong hands caught her around the waist and pulled her up. Parker. She still couldn't stand on her own, though. If he wasn't holding her, she'd have fallen into the grass again.

"Are you all right?" he asked. The concern, almost panic, she heard in his voice reached her.

Giving herself up, she slumped against Parker's solid frame. He hugged her close, whispering in her ear and holding her tight. She felt his mouth kiss her forehead and she began to breathe easier, but she still clung to him. His hands caressed her back, moving in circles as he held her securely against his chest.

McKenna wasn't sure how long they stood like that. Eventually Parker released her, yet was keeping her close to him, probably until the shock wore off.

"I'm okay now," she said, pushing away. "I need to check the car."

"Give yourself some time. You've had a shock."

"So have you."

He nodded. "We kept each other together."

McKenna knew he was giving her some credit, though he was stronger than she was. He'd offered soothing words until she was back to normal. Whatever normal was after an accident.

"I never even saw those deer. They came out of nowhere."

"The trees obscured them. It was impossible to see either one coming. But you kept the car from flipping over. It could have been worse—much worse."

"It's getting dark. We won't be able to see much in a few minutes."

"We can look at the damage in the morning. The last sign we passed said it was forty miles to Catoosa. Too far to walk anywhere. And in the darkness no one will expect us to be walking on the road. It's too dangerous to try it. Like it or not, we're going to have to spend the night in this field."

Darkness fell quickly and soon they could see nothing except the stars overhead. No moon hung in the sky.

"When I was ten, I wanted to sleep outside like this," Parker said, seemingly out of the blue.

"Really?" McKenna asked.

"It's so freeing out here. I remember that night, the same feeling, when my brother and I came up with the idea."

"Camping out in your backyard?"

"Yep," he replied. "My brother and I tried to talk my father into letting us do it, but he said no. 'A silly and unnecessary idea,' he insisted. I guess I'll get my chance tonight."

Parker burrowed down into the grass. McKenna's attitude toward him softened. It was the first time he'd said anything that led her to believe his childhood might not have been as idyllic as she'd assumed. McKenna's childhood had been almost perfect. Until her parents' death, she'd grown up loved and supported in whatever she wanted to do. Her father had driven her to sporting events, piano lessons. Her mother handled soccer, tennis and horseback riding. Both attended the school plays, parents' nights and cheered for her on the school's basketball team.

She knew there were more unfortunate kids, people with real problems like drugs and neglect. She could sympathize with Joanna's situation, but that wasn't how she had grown up. She was lucky.

McKenna knew she shouldn't infer anything about Parker's childhood on the strength of a single comment, but the tone he used had her curious. Had his home life been like hers or more difficult? McKenna was unsure.

Thoughts of Joanna came back to her. Had Parker recognized a need in her because he worked with teenagers all the time, or was it something more personal in his makeup that had alerted him?

AFTER A FEW MINUTES of looking at the sky, Parker got up and headed for the car.

"Where are you going?" McKenna asked.

"To get the blankets. You're getting cold."

In the emergency kit in the trunk were two blankets. McKenna must have added a second one for Lydia. He loved that she planned for unexpected contingencies.

Closing the trunk he saw she'd twisted around to watch him. She was changing toward him. Not long ago, she wouldn't even look in his direction. Now she had a smile on her face.

Going to her, he placed a blanket around her shoulders and spread the other one on the ground. McKenna leaned against a tree. Parker stretched out and watched her.

"Are you enjoying this trip?" he asked.

"Absolutely," she said without hesitation.

"Even this part? The car breaking down and us stranded in the middle of nowhere?"

He could barely see her with the light fading so quickly, but he thought her face was glowing. She'd pulled her hair free of the band she used when driving to keep it out of her face. The frame softened her features.

"Even this." She glanced around, then brought her attention back to him. "Have I told you I'm glad I'm not alone?"

"Once or twice." He laughed.

"Have you thought about home? What's going on back there?"

Until she'd asked, Parker hadn't considered anything in Chicago. Often he thought of her. She was with him. This was the trip of a lifetime in his eyes. Nothing mattered if she wasn't there.

"I'm sure everyone back there is fine," he said. "They're probably wondering what we're doing."

"Wouldn't they be surprised to find out we're going to sleep in a field and that we're no longer fighting?"

The sun was totally gone now and the night was pitch black. "Do you still want to fight with me?" he asked.

"No," McKenna said.

Her voice was disembodied, but not unnatural. Parker faced her, getting a little closer as the darkness enveloped them.

The universe grew larger overhead, but his world sat only a few feet from him. Coming on this trip had been a good idea, despite his misgivings. McKenna was getting to know him. He wanted her to know him. Not the person she'd avoided in the past, but who he was today.

Still, each time she mentioned Marshall it seemed she pulled back.

By now, he thought she'd have realized the truth of Marshall's death and Parker's role in it.

CHAPTER TEN

MCKENNA WAS AWED by the number of stars overhead. She could see only a few in her Woodbine Heights neighborhood. The spillage of light from Chicago bled the sky so white it obscured the stars. But here in this field, miles from the concrete jungle, she appreciated the heavens.

Glancing sideways, she saw Parker had his eyes closed. The wonder of the universe was playing out above his head and he chose to sleep. Was he really sleeping, or had the events of the last couple of hours taken a toll on him and he was hiding it from her?

"Parker, are you asleep?" His eyes opened and she breathed a sigh of relief. "How's your neck?"

"It's a little sore."

The car had seat belts, but no shoulder harnesses.

"I was afraid you might have a concussion."

"I didn't hit my head that hard. It's all right to go to sleep. Things will be clearer in the morning."

The night sounds disturbed her. She was used to hearing police sirens, street traffic, but the cicadas and crickets made her think of spiders and other crawling insects. Besides those sounds, the place was absolutely silent.

McKenna's day had been traumatic. She was glad Parker was with her, she had to admit. She didn't want to be alone and facing uncertainty. She concentrated on the stars, trying to find the Big Dipper and the other constellations that she could identify from their proximity to them. But they blurred. She wiped her eyes and tried again. It was too hard and her neck did hurt. She didn't tell Parker, because he would worry, maybe even insist they use his cell phone to call help. The last things she wanted was to end this trip in a hospital emergency room.

Closing her eyes she practiced a relaxation technique Marshall had taught her to reduce or shut down an ache without medi-cation. After a while, her mind cleared and she drifted off to sleep, only to be awakened by a burning pain.

THE NOISE JOLTED PARKER. Opening his eyes, he immediately searched for McKenna. She was writhing, her hands working feverishly over her arms as she sat in the early dawn light.

In seconds he was beside her. He saw what caused her distress. Red ants were making breakfast out of her skin. With-out thinking, he started scraping his hands down her body, pushing away the insects. She was covered in them. Grabbing her arm, he pulled her away from the apparent nest.

Still, they were all over her. Ripping his T-shirt over his head, Parker used it to brush away the offending creatures. She did the same with her shirt before throwing it to-ward the disabled car. Her shorts followed the shirt. Her body was covered in red welts.

"Don't scratch," he said. "You'll make it worse."

Her face contorted and she grabbed his

upper arms. Hanging on for support, her fingers dug into his bare skin. Her head fell back as agony showed on her face. He felt the heat of her hands. His skin burned where she touched him. "We need to get you something for the pain and itch," he growled.

There was a first-aid kit in the car. He wanted to get it, but McKenna had her arms imprisoning him. He broke her grip, even though he was reluctant to do so. He was unsure what red ants would do to a person. Were they poisonous? His heart beat faster at the thought that McKenna might be in danger.

He used some anti-itch medication on the red welts that marred her back and legs. Working as if he were a doctor, he spread the cream down her back and over her arms and legs. Parker applied the stuff liberally. They would have to get more at a drugstore as soon as the car was working. He hoped there were no permanent aftereffects, but he would feel a lot better if she saw a doctor.

"You'll have to use this on your chest," he told her, holding the tube out to her. She took it, squeezed a generous portion into her palm and spread it over her neck and lower down.

Parker turned away. He wouldn't watch her. It would be wrong, especially knowing how he felt about her. Going to the car, he pulled clean clothes from her backpack and handed them to her.

"Why didn't they attack you?" she asked, quickly dressing. The sun rose and even with her pain, she was cognizant of standing half-dressed in a field.

"Apparently, you were lying too close to their nest. I was several feet away. Are you feeling any better?" he asked.

"Well, the pain everywhere else made me forget about my neck."

"What about your neck?"

"Whiplash. Don't you have it, too?"

"The deer was more on your side of the car, so you had the greater impact than I did." He checked the first-aid kit for aspirin. There was none.

Parker checked their surroundings. There was nothing around them. No farmhouse in the distance. No friendly neighbors to call on for assistance. "I think we've reached the point of calling this an emergency," he told her. "I'll need to use the phone to at least call Triple-A for assistance."

McKenna cocked her head. Parker listened, too. He heard nothing.

"There it is again," she said. "It's a car. No, a truck." She took a step toward the direction of the sound, this time Parker heard it, too. "By the pitch of the engine I'd say it's a Dodge Ram. A fairly recent model, no more than two or three years old."

Both rushed to the edge of the field just as a blue Dodge Ram came over the rise. McKenna stepped onto the road and waved her arms. She quickly put one down and Parker understood that she felt pain in her neck.

"Lost?" the man said when he stopped the truck.

"Accident," Parker said. "We need a tow truck. Is there one in a town nearby?"

"Nearest town is forty miles away. But I can call one for you." He picked up a phone and flipped through several numbers. "Where's the car?"

McKenna pointed over to where the Corvette sat.

"Hmm," he said. "Did you hit something?"

"A deer."

"They can sure kill a car," he said. Then someone answered on the other end and he began to talk. "Zeke, this is Paul. I'm out on the 66 where the Milhouses used to live. Been an accident. Need a tow." He listened a moment. Then he looked at them. "Either of you hurt?"

"A little whiplash and the lady had a run-in with some ants."

"Minor," he said into the phone. Again he listened, and then said, "It looks like a sports car, low to ground, restored by the looks of it. How long before you can get here?" Pushing the phone away from his mouth, he asked if two hours was agreeable.

"We've waited all night. Two hours is fine," Parker said.

"Okay, Zeke. And bring food for two. They've been here all night." He hung up. "Zeke'll be here soon. I'd take you myself, but I'm heading in the other direction."

"Thank you," McKenna said. "You've been very helpful."

Parker shook hands with the man. "I'm Parker Fordum. This is McKenna Wellington."

"Nice to meet you both. Be careful of those ants, and Zeke'll be here soon."

They stepped back from the truck and Paul waved as he continued on this way.

"People actually stopping to help a stranger on the road." Parker shook his head. "Will wonders never cease?"

"Hello," McKenna called, holding on to the last syllable as if it was the last note of a song. The cavernous space was dark inside the garage and gas station. "Anybody here?"

She heard the scraping of wheels and saw a man pulling himself out from under a 1939 Studebaker. If she hadn't known cars, she'd wonder who would want a car that old. But seeing it instantly gave her hope that vintage cars might be the mechanic's specialty.

"Can I help you?" He didn't rise, rather he stayed on his back. She saw he was lying on a makeshift pallet. Apparently, cars weren't the only thing old in this garage.

"I need some help. My car broke down a few miles back on Route 66."

He sat up. McKenna saw his hair poking out from a baseball cap that he had on backward. Equal parts of red and grey extended past his ears and rested on thin shoulders. His face was craggy from years in the sun and his teeth were stained yellow, probably from a lifetime of coffee and cigarettes.

"Didn't Andy come and get you?"

Andy drove the tow truck, which was right out of the animated movie *Cars*. The tow truck was old and rusted and McKenna was unsure it would make it the forty miles to Catoosa. The incongruity of a Corvette hooked to its winch was as cartoonish as the movie. The driver wore navy blue overalls that looked as if they hadn't been washed in years. The name Zeke was sewn into his top pocket, but his name was Andy.

"He brought us in a few minutes ago. He said I'd find Zeke under a car. Are you Zeke?"

"I am."

"Well, I'm sure my car needs a water pump."

He raised a single eyebrow. McKenna recognized the cynicism in the move. In the circles she traveled in, no one looked at her as if she didn't know what she was talking about when it came to any type of vehicle, and that included tractor-trailers and plain old farm equipment. She could take an engine apart and put it back together in her sleep. But outside her community she was just a pretty little lady who knew nothing from nothing.

"Do you have time to look at it? Maybe give me an estimate?"

"There are a couple of cars in front of yours. Their owners are just as anxious as you are."

"If you have a water pump, I'll fix it myself."

"Against the rules," he said.

McKenna sighed. "Anyplace I can get a cup of coffee while I wait?"

"Diner, four blocks west." He pointed to his right in case she couldn't read the sun or the road sign right next to the station's driveway. "If you want something any fancier, you'll have to get on the highway and drive fifteen or so miles to Tulsa." He laughed then and McKenna joined him.

"I think the diner will be fine."

He lay back and started to roll under the car again when she stopped him.

"Don't you want to know what car it is?" she asked.

"I imagine it's the only flashy sportscar out there? Not many of those flying by on the 66."

Exactly. And given the previous reception she'd gotten with the car, McKenna decided to play her trump card. "It's a red-and-white 1959 Corvette Stingray."

The man's motion stopped abruptly and he rolled himself forward again.

"Convertible?" he asked.

"Why have a Corvette if you can't let the top down?" Again they both smiled. "Since you're working on a Studebaker, '39 by my guess, I figured you'd be familiar with another vintage car."

He pointed at the car. "This one's mine, but a Studebaker is not a 'Vette."

"The concept is the same," McKenna said.

"Never worked on one. You'd do better

taking it to a dealer, but even they might not have the parts for a '59."

"It's just a water pump."

He frowned. "Could be a radiator. Could be something else."

She shook her head. "It's the pump."

"Even if it is, we don't have it."

"What about a bay? I can start with a tune-up until the part gets here. " She looked down the space. There was a truck in the next bay, but the last one was empty.

He took a moment to stand up and stared at her from head to toe. "What happened to you?"

"Ants. We had to spend the night in a field. Unfortunately, the ants didn't like me invading their home." McKenna still itched from her encounter. She forced herself not to scratch.

"Better get something to put on that."

"I did. I will. I see a drugstore right down the street. I'll go there. But, before I leave, what about the bay?"

"Never seen a lady mechanic. Other than on television, that is. Or you got a man to do the work?"

Immediately her thoughts ran to Parker.

She did have a man with her, but saying she had a man was too weird an implication.

"I do the work," she answered.

He removed his backward ballcap and ran his hand through his long, greasy locks before replacing it.

"You know your way around cars or are you pulling my leg?"

McKenna raised her hand in the girl scout salute. "I promise I'm familiar with cars. I built that little number outside from the garage floor up."

He went to the door and looked out. Andy had lowered the car from the back of the tow truck.

"She's a beauty," Zeke said.

"The accident caused a small crack in the front left fender. And the water pump is busted. I haven't been under it yet, but my instincts are rarely wrong."

Crossing his arms, he leaned back on his heels. "You talk a good game, but that still don't prove you know what you're doing. I have insurance to be concerned about, and it won't cover an amateur getting hurt in here."

"I'll sign a waiver. If I get hurt it's on me."

He thought for a moment, still with his arms crossed and still looking out at the red and white car. "I guess it'll be all right."

McKenna almost jumped for joy. She hadn't had her hands in a car since she finished working on the Corvette. She had discovered she loved doing it. It made her realize now that she had done it for herself, and not Marshall. It was hers, her creation and hers alone. Not even her husband or his memory could claim ownership of a single screw, rivet or part.

"What's your name?" Zeke asked.

"McKenna Wellington," she said.

"Wellington?" He uncrossed his arms and stood up straight. His eyes bored into hers. "You're McKenna Wellington, owner of M and M Wellington Parts and Tools?"

"Guilty," she said, twisting her mouth to the side. She never expected to be recognized. Hers wasn't a household name.

"Well, why didn't you say so?"

"You know who I am?" she asked.

He moved back into the garage, going to a desk in the corner that was littered with parts, books, paper coffee cups and tools. Rifling through the debris, he came up with a three-year-old trade magazine. Holding it up to her, she saw herself dressed in a white suit and standing between a royal blue Chevrolet and a cherry-red Ford. New Models Roll Off the Assembly Line was the caption. A couple of coffee rings stained the cover and the cars weren't so brightly colored anymore. The story went on to talk about her taking over as the sole head of the company after Marshall's death.

"Amazing," Zeke said, his smile even wider now. "Of course you can work in one of the bays. We'll get your car on the lift. You do everything else."

"Is there a rental charge for the bay?"

"As my first lady mechanic, and for the honor of having you on-site, the bay is yours, along with any tools that I'm not using. Course, we still don't have a water pump for a '59 Corvette. You're going to have to order one, and that will take some time."

"Deal," she said, extending her hand.

He looked at her long fingers, then at his dirty ones. "Maybe we'd better shake on it later."

"As a lady mechanic," she said. "I've had grease more places than on my hands."

She took his and shook it.

"Now, what are you doing to that Studebaker?"

USING ZEKE'S DIRECTIONS, Parker found McKenna at the diner. He slipped into the booth across from her.

"I found a job," Parker said. Even he recognized the pride evident in his voice.

McKenna's eyes widened. Before she could ask a question, the waitress arrived with a pot of coffee in each hand.

She filled Parker's cup, but then left. He was confused.

"Didn't she want our order?" Parker asked.

"I ordered for us both," McKenna stated.

Parker's brows rose. Had she learned enough about his likes and dislikes to actually do that?

It was something couples did, he realized. Eating with McKenna for weeks now, he'd seen her choices. Obviously, she'd noted his, too.

"Where's the job? Doing what?" She smiled and perked up.

"First, I tried for short order cook here, but apparently, they have enough staff."

"Even with Sherry's glowing recommendation, you didn't get the job?" she teased.

"Even with that. However, I scored something better," Parker said. "At least, it pays better."

"Good," McKenna said. "Because a water pump for that car is going to cost at least five hundred dollars. And we have to order it."

Parker whistled. "Which means we'll be stuck here awhile."

"Quick study, I like that." McKenna chuckled.

She'd begun to joke with him. They sure were back on friendly terms. He hoped it would last.

"Tell me about this job. What is it? When do you start?"

"Tomorrow. In a warehouse. There's a factory at the edge of town. It's a good walk from here, but I won't need transportation."

"What will you be doing?"

"I'll be loading boxes on a pallet. Then a crane comes and loads them onto a truck."

"For eight hours a day?" Her voice was at least an octave higher.

"If I'm lucky."

"Parker, that's a college student's summer job."

"True, that's why I got it. They needed help and not enough students applied."

She looked down, as if guilty.

"What's wrong? I thought you'd be happy. We get towed into town and within an hour, I have employment. We should be celebrating." He lifted the cup of coffee the waitress had set in front of him the moment he'd reached the booth.

"Parker, you didn't sign on for this. You're thirty years old. You have a doctorate in Economics. And you're going to be doing manual labor?"

"I'm happy to help," he said. "And just think, I'll be more in touch with my students when we return to Chicago."

He was attempting to make light of their situation. He appreciated what McKenna was saying, but she was overreacting.

"I'll see what kind of work I can get.

Maybe they need a waitress." She tried to laugh, but failed.

"We're sticking to our plan," Parker reassured her.

It suddenly occurred to him that he'd said *our* plan and not *her* plan.

"McKenna, we said if we needed to work to make enough money to go on, that's what we would do."

"Have you ever done manual labor before?"

"You don't think working at Sherry's was manual labor?" Parker smiled, hoping she'd catch on to his teasing.

"That's different from doing the exact same thing over and over for one-third of your day."

"I've never packed and moved boxes for an extended period of time, but I've done my share of lifting and carrying. I'll be able to hold my own," he told her. "It's not your fault. You didn't break the water pump."

"I know, but I have to fix it and you've gotten a job to take care of me."

She didn't know how much he wanted to take care of her. "Only temporarily until you find a job. Besides, you'd do the same for me if our roles were reversed."

Her eyes stared into his. The truth of his words seemed to reach them both at the same time.

He reached over and squeezed her hand, the gesture telling her everything would be fine. Then he let go and sat back.

The waitress brought their food. Both he and McKenna were quiet until their server moved on to the next booth.

"Aren't you going to smile?" Parker teased again.

"The food looks good," McKenna said, giving him a weak smile.

They ate in silence. Parker enjoyed the lunch she'd ordered for him. It was an open-faced turkey sandwich with broccoli and sweet potatoes. It was something he liked and it tasted better knowing that McKenna had spotted his preferences.

He felt fairly certain he would have chosen for her the spaghetti, salad and iced tea she seemed to be enjoying.

Both refused dessert when the waitress removed their plates, but McKenna ordered coffee and Parker had his cup refilled. He wondered if McKenna was struggling with something. She seemed preoccupied.

She leaned forward, putting her chin in her palm and looked through the window. He glanced outside. Few people were on the street. Cars were angle parked along the curb.

"You're not still brooding over the job, are you?" Parker asked.

HE NOTICED HER HANDS. And here McKenna thought the red welts she had were less raw-looking.

She stared at Parker's hands, recalling how soft they'd been as he'd cleared the ants from her and then applied the cream to help soothe her skin. She considered how different his hands would be after a few weeks spent in the warehouse.

McKenna had worked shifts in the warehouse that she and Marshall owned. She'd done every facet of every job to get their business going. Initially, she'd been run off her feet picking, packing and shipping parts during the internet-only phase of their business. Now they had bricks and mortar stores as well as their online sales. Teams of people were employed to do what she and Marshall used to tackle on their own.

"Are you still in pain?" Parker asked.

McKenna wore a long-sleeved blouse, so no one could spot the angry marks on her arms. "I stopped at the drugstore and bought some hydrocortisone. It's made the swelling go down some and the itch isn't as bad."

Parker drained the last of his coffee. Her cup was empty.

"We'd better go and find a room for the night. We don't want to spend it in another field."

He slid sideways on the bench seat, preparing to get up. McKenna knew she had to talk to him. And it had to be now.

CHAPTER ELEVEN

OUT IN THE SUNSHINE, Parker said, "I asked about a bed-and-breakfast or a motel in town. I got the names of several that are relatively close by."

He stopped and reached into his pocket. McKenna watched as he pulled out a piece of paper that contained the information.

"If my directions are correct, the first one is about three streets down."

They walked the short distance, checking for street names and addresses until the found the bed-and-breakfast. It was a huge Victorian house with a wide wraparound porch and big windows.

McKenna stopped Parker next to a short chain link fence. "Parker, do you mind if I bring up a touchy subject?"

She watched his shoulders stiffen. He

stood up straighter as if bracing himself for some kind of blow.

"What is it?"

"You can say no and I'll abide by your decision."

"This is very intriguing, but what is it?" His tone was a little harder than she thought it should be.

"You know when we were working at Sherry's and we decided that we had enough money to get separate rooms?"

"Yes," he replied, elongating the word.

"I've been thinking and doing some financial calculations in my head." She swallowed. This was more difficult than she thought it would be. She'd never asked a man to share with her before.

"I thought economics was my job." She could tell by his grin that he was attempting to lighten the mood.

"It is sort of economics. The economics of this trip and its future. There are a few things we want to do as we travel this road. Some of them a bit expensive."

Again he nodded, but remained silent.

"If we are to accomplish them, we'll need to be frugal in our spending."

"We've been doing that from the beginning."

"We have, but it's not going to work if we continue to spend money on separate rooms."

A breath seemed to whoosh out of him.

"You can say no." McKenna rushed the words, thinking he might consider it going backward. He was protective of her, but he might also want his privacy. "It's all right. We can get jobs and make a little more money. I shouldn't have brought it up."

"McKenna." He tried to break into her tirade, but she continued as if he hadn't spoken.

"It was a bad idea. You do probably want your privacy, and I keep you from being free to do what you want."

"McKenna!"

She stopped talking and looked at him, her eyes wide in surprise at the strength of his voice.

"I haven't said no."

"Is that a yes?" she almost whispered.

"We should discuss this, understand what we're doing and what we're asking of each other."

"I'm only asking that we manage the money we have or can earn wisely until the trip is over."

Parker was frowning as she spoke. "We've already passed a point in our relationship and we can't undo it."

"What are you talking about?"

"Would you like me to show you?" he asked.

She stepped back as if he might take her in his arms and kiss her the way he had before. She felt the heat flashing through her body.

"I see you do."

"We already talked about that kiss," McKenna told him. "I am aware there's an attraction between us. But it won't work and we both know it. I'm only bringing up the subject because we've had a couple of snags so far and I really want this trip to work." She waited a moment for him to challenge her on snags. When he nodded in agreement, she went on. "Financially, I don't think we have a choice."

"I understand," he said. "If we don't take measures to change things, we'll be on this road until winter."

McKenna didn't appreciate the manner in which he said that, but she thought she might have heard a yes buried in that comment.

"Okay, so for the record, when we go inside, do we want two rooms, or one room with two beds? Whatever you feel comfortable with is what we'll do." She was going to let him make the decision.

"I'm sure proximity to you won't kill me." He took her arm and she winced. "I'm sorry. I forgot about your pain." He let her go. "Did I hurt you?"

McKenna shook her head. At that moment she would try to speak. Had he hurt her? Somehow the answer to that question was yes.

As PARKER HEADED off to work at the warehouse the next morning, McKenna went to the garage. Her car was no longer sitting where she'd left it. Her heart lurched and she began to run. She reached the first two bays, but the doors were down and she couldn't see inside. Winded, she rushed inside.

"Zeke," she called, panic in her voice. She and Parker had been robbed before. She had thoughts that someone had taken the car.

"Over here," he called back.

McKenna faced the sound and saw Zeke at the back of the garage with a cup of coffee in his hand.

"Where's my car?"

"Where do you think it is? I told you that you could use the last bay."

She looked toward it. The truck that was in bay two still sat there. She walked behind it and saw the lift in bay three had been raised.

"I thought you'd want to check the undercarriage." Zeke spoke from beside her. "I looked at it. I don't see anything. If you only drove across the grass at the old Milhouse place, then I don't think you could do much damage if you didn't hit a rock or a tree."

McKenna confirmed that neither of those mishaps had occurred.

"Go on and check it out." He gestured with his coffee.

With a smile that lifted her spirits, McKenna went to the car. There was nothing pouring out of it: no oil, antifreeze, brake fluid or transmission fluid. No danger hung from the downpipe and nothing was loose. Zeke had raised the car for his height which was only a few inches taller than her five-foot-five-inch frame. Her skin was tight over the disappearing welts. Stretching could be uncomfortable.

Lowering the car to a point where she could see and reach it, she inspected it for cracks, holes, breaks and leaks. Running her hand over the pipes, she checked for anything she couldn't see but might be able to feel. Other than pulling away errant grass, all was intact.

"Thank the universe," she said out loud. She could use some good news. Last night she and Parker were back in the same room, but unlike their sharing after the robbery, there was a strain between them. Both knew they had no choice and she had to say he was taking it well. Maybe better than she was.

Several times during the night, she wanted to get up and apologize to him. Thoughts of heading back to Chicago or using their credit cards came to her.

What was she really doing this trip for? What did she have to prove and who was she proving it to? It wasn't for Marshall. She already knew that. Even if it was, he was gone and there was no way she could let him know that she was fulfilling one of his dreams. This was her dream, but she didn't have to do it this way. Parker had logical reasons for them traveling using the conveniences of today, not just what existed in the 1960s.

She liked traveling Route 66. She was glad she'd chosen it. Sure, it was a slower ride, but it gave her more time with…she stopped. She was about to say more time with Parker.

Why did that matter?

It didn't matter, she told herself. They were traveling as fast as the quality of the road allowed. Visiting some of the sights along the route and meeting people were high on her to-do list, and she wanted to do more than say hello and goodbye. So far circumstances had allowed them to do that without trying.

Finding the control to lower the car, McKenna saw a red tool chest. The multilevel drawers were open at various stages. Inside there looked to be a full set of tools. Lying next to the tool chest was a clean set of blue coveralls. They had Zeke stitched over the pocket in white thread. McKenna whipped around and looked for Zeke.

He was just returning to the garage. She heard the click of a bell indicating someone was leaving the gas pumps.

"Zeke," she shouted to him, holding the coveralls.

He spotted her and started toward her. "Try them on. They won't fit, but they'll save your clothes."

McKenna slipped easily into the jumpsuit and slipped the sleeves along her arms and over her shoulders to protect what she was wearing.

"You are a sweetheart," she said.

"Don't tell anybody. I got a rep to maintain."

McKenna laughed. Zeke's craggy, sun-burned face broke into a grin.

"I did some checking last night on a water pump for this type of car. Can't find one. I even tried online. You can usually find anything there."

"How about a junkyard? Are there any around here?"

"Not close by. Must be a hundred miles to the nearest car yard. Where'd you get this one from?" He pointed to the car.

"I have some sources. Is it all right if I use your phone? It's an 800 number, so there won't be a charge."

"It's in the office." He led her to a room made of half windows and half wood—at least it was once wood. Now it was more oil-stained wallboard. Inside his office, she found a phone that must have been original to the day the building opened for business. It was black, weighed at least fifteen pounds and had a dial she had to put her fingers in and turn. There was a dial tone and when a voice answered on the other end, the sound was as clear as if she was speaking to someone next door.

Within ten minutes she'd ordered the part. Looking at an invoice on the desk for a shipment of gaskets, she saw the address of the garage and gave it to the clerk she'd dealt with on much of the Corvette's restoration. Then, breaking protocol, she had the cost of it put on the M and M Wellington Parts and Tools account. She had to consider this an emergency. If they didn't get the pump fixed, they couldn't leave Oklahoma. She'd reimburse her business account as soon as she could.

As she left the office, a car pulled up to the full service gas pumps. She glanced around for Zeke or an attendant, but didn't see anyone. McKenna knew how to work the pumps. She provided the gas, accepted a credit card payment and gave a receipt to the driver. Everything else was taken care of by the internal mechanism of the gas pump.

By the time Zeke came within view again, she'd seen to three cars in need of gas, and stood back for a truck that was pulling in. The truck stopped at the self-service pump and got out.

"Paul," she called as she recognized him.

"Well, hello again."

She reached out and shook hands with him.

"How did you make out?" he asked.

"We'll be here for a while. Car needs a water pump. I had to order it, so it's a waiting game until then."

Zeke joined them. The two men acknowledged each other.

"Are you working here?" Paul asked staring at her clothes.

"Yes," she said.

"Paul, I suppose you don't know who this is," Zeke asked.

Paul looked at McKenna closely without recognition. "Other than she was a stranded motorist, no." The pump clicked. Paul moved to it and pulled the nozzle free. He reseated it in its cradle and waited for his receipt. "So, who are you?"

Zeke answered, "This is McKenna Wellington."

The name didn't register for Paul.

"She's the owner of M and M Wellington Parts and Tools."

"Really." Paul's brows rose. "I've used a

few of those in my time. I never knew it was owned by a woman."

"My husband and I owned it. He died a few years ago."

Again Paul frowned. "Parker," he said, seemingly searching for the name. "I thought you two were married."

She shook her head. "We're traveling together, taking Route 66 all the way to the coast. He's working at the factory."

"That was fast," he said.

"They needed help. Apparently, he was in the right place at the right time."

He nodded as if he understood something, when McKenna knew he had no idea about their relationship. The truth was, neither did she.

MᴄKᴇɴɴᴀ ᴡᴀs at her wits' end. So far Paul and Zeke were the only people she knew here other than Parker. She didn't know what to do to fill all the hours. The part wouldn't arrive for at least three days, maybe a week. In the meantime, she'd pumped gas and talked to several people who were surprised to find her employed by Zeke. She wasn't working for him, technically. She was helping out. But maybe she should look for a real job.

Zeke went to get some lunch and she was alone in the gas station. Business was slow. Walking into the bay where Zeke had his Studebaker, she wandered over to the car. Like her, he was restoring the 1939 vintage automobile to its former glory. He didn't have an engine in it, so he still had a long way to go.

"Hello," someone called.

McKenna turned around. "Here," she said. "Need some gas?" She started walking toward a man in a suit. McKenna didn't often classify people, but this man fit a type.

He was clean cut. His hair was perfect, not a strand out of place. Not a smudge nor a wrinkle. He was someone who likely went to a men's salon rather than a barber. He probably drove a BMW or a Maserati. Although she wouldn't be surprised to find a Silver Cloud parked outside the bay door and him asking where the local classic car dealer could be found.

"I need some service, not gas. Is there a

mechanic here? My car is making a funny sound."

"He's not here at the moment. Tell me what's wrong and I'll see if I can help you."

"You're Zeke?" he questioned.

McKenna had a flashback to asking the same question and smiled. "No, but I can help you out," she said. "Now, what's the funny noise?"

"It's coming from the front. I can't tell if it's on the right or the left. It's a crunching er-er-er sound."

"When does it happen?"

"When I'm driving over forty miles an hour. It doesn't happen under that."

"What about turning?" she asked.

"Doesn't happen then, either."

She walked outside. He fell into step with her. Sitting next to the open bay was a Jaguar. It was a work of art.

"This is a very expensive car," he began, confirming McKenna's assessment of him.

"I know," she said. "It's a Jaguar F-Type silver coupé, 2014, I'd guess."

"You know cars?" He looked at the antiquated garage.

"A few things," she said, noncommittal on purpose. "From your description, it sounds like you need your wheel bearings repacked."

"You haven't even looked at the car."

"I'm sure that's your problem. You can still drive it, but it'll wear your tires and reduce your gas mileage."

"Do you know where there's a Jag dealer or a classic car repair shop?"

"Not a clue," she said. "But I'm sure you have a device that will search and find the nearest one. Oklahoma City is 120 miles southwest of here. There's a very good one there."

"Will the car make it?"

"I can't say without taking the tire off and looking at the bearing. The noise will continue if you drive it. You could make it, or you could have a tire blow. It depends on how bad the bearing is."

His expression showed the dilemma was weighing on him. "I've never had anyone work on my car except a certified Jag tech."

"There is another option."

"What's that?"

"Towing."

His face scrunched into a mask. "Tow it 120 miles."

McKenna understood. It wasn't the distance or the cost. It was him sitting in a tow truck for more than two hours in his thousand-dollar suit.

"I take it you don't have the parts here."

"I doubt it. The bearing can be repacked, then you can take it to Oklahoma City and have it redone or replaced."

He didn't seem to like that option, either.

"You sure there isn't anyone else here?"

"By anyone, you mean any *man* here?"

"Frankly, yes."

"I'm sure. I can spot a man from a mile away." At that point, she saw Zeke crossing the street. "Look, here comes one now."

The man followed her gaze. Zeke carried a brown paper bag and had a cup holder with two cups of what looked like soft drinks balanced in his right hand.

"Zeke, this guy is looking for a man who knows cars."

Zeke looked at the Jag and then at the well-suited man. "How can I help you?"

"The lady says I need bearings."

"Wheel noise at high speeds, doesn't happen on turns or when you're going slow."

The guy nodded, smiling for the first time.

"She's right. It's probably the bearings. Need to look in the wheel to find out for sure." He turned to McKenna. "Here's your lunch."

She took the bag and the drinks and headed for the office. Before she got to the door, she heard Zeke tell the guy. "Want me to take a look at it?"

"Have you ever worked on a Jag?"

"Nope, but the lady's been under more cars than you can count, including Jags."

She smiled and closed the door.

THE MILE-AND-A-HALF WALK back to the B&B was more than Parker thought he could handle after finishing his first day in a factory. He'd grown up and gone through school with the intention of being a teacher. Finding he didn't like hormonal teenagers, he worked on his masters and PhD and taught college. That setting was perfect for him.

Summer jobs were in offices apart from his one experience as a short order cook. Nothing he'd done was equal to the back-breaking work of loading and stacking boxes. He now understood why this job was available when he'd gone to the factory asking for work.

Parker picked up one foot and put it down, then the other. Each step felt as if his legs were weighed down with lead. His back and neck hurt. He truly sympathized with how McKenna felt with ant welts all over her body. However, he didn't think there was any cream strong enough that he could buy to help soothe his soreness—it was that bad.

He had to pass the garage where McKenna left the Corvette for repair. When he reached the place, he'd rest awhile before continuing. It took him longer to get there than expected.

"Hi, Parker." McKenna's chipper voice stopped him. He almost stumbled, but that would make it even harder to go on. She sounded happy and…fresh, but even more surprising was seeing her dressed in coveralls, wearing gloves and her body bent under the hood of a car.

"McKenna," he replied, frowning, forgetting his own pain. "What are you doing?"

"I was just helping Zeke out."

He eyed her from head to foot.

"He lent me the coveralls."

"And I hired her." Zeke came from around the other side of the car. "Do you know what a wizard she is with these tools?"

Parker didn't. He knew her ability only by reputation and by the car they'd driven since leaving Chicago.

"We even had a Jaguar in here today."

He looked to McKenna. "A guy from the highway needed bearings repacked."

"I thought Jag owners only went to Jag service centers.'

"True," Zeke said.

"The nearest dealer is 120 miles away. So Zeke convinced him to let me look at it." She placed what looked like a small wrench into a toolbox. "I'm sure he was going to the dealer as soon as he left here, but I made sure the car could make it without the trouble he described."

"Sounds like you had a wonderful day."

"I did, but it's time to knock off. Wait

right here." Pulling off the gloves, she placed them on a cabinet. "I'll go wash my hands. I have dinner all ready. I thought you might be tired."

She left without a comment from him. Both Parker and Zeke watched her leave.

"I never thought I'd see a lady mechanic," Zeke commented. "You got a good one there." He winked conspiratorially.

Parker moved his attention from watching McKenna to Zeke. Did the guy think they were a couple, even if they weren't married? What had McKenna told him about their relationship?

"I know," Parker replied.

CHAPTER TWELVE

ENTERING THE B&B, McKenna went straight to the shower and washed her hair. She'd used the special cleansing soap at Zeke's for her hands, but she needed to rid herself of any residual oil.

Parker showered after McKenna. He stayed in the bathroom a long time. He'd looked tired and McKenna knew his muscles had to be aching, but he was doing a good job of hiding it.

When he came out of the bathroom, she had dinner set out on the small table. He was dressed in clean shorts and a short-sleeved shirt.

"What are we having?" he asked.

"Sandwiches, soft drinks, followed by a massage and a rubdown."

"What?"

"You can try to hide it, but I know how

you normally walk and what you're doing is an imitation of it." He gave her that not-quite-lopsided grin and McKenna changed the subject. "How was the day?"

"Grueling." His voice was serious and honest. He took a seat across from her at the table. "It was worse than you said. I never stacked so many boxes in my life."

"Just think of the muscles you'll build," she teased. He'd lifted and carried her. He'd kissed her. She'd felt the strength of him. The last thing he needed was more muscles.

Parker devoured his food, further confirmation that he'd worked like a horse. She gave him credit, however. He'd stayed the whole day and then dead on his feet started walking to the B&B. Despite his tough attitude, it was lucky that Zeke had driven them the last half mile here.

McKenna got up and took an extra blanket from the closet shelf. Spreading it on the floor, she made a large enough space. "Come on, lie down on your stomach."

"I'm all right. I don't need a massage," Parker protested.

"Liar," she said. "Your muscles need

stretching or you'll be useless tomorrow. Take off the shirt and lie down."

Reluctantly, he did as she instructed. When she reached for his shoulders, Parker jumped. His entire body stiffened. "Sorry," she said. "My hands are a little cold." She tried again, determined to help him get rid of some of the strain the day had caused.

"I broke protocol today," she told him, her hands working his shoulders.

"You what?" Parker turned his head to look at her.

She kept focused on her task. "I ordered the pump. It'll be here in a few days if all goes well. Though it might take as long as a week."

"How did you break protocol?"

"I charged the cost of the part to the Wellington account. I surmised that needing the part constituted an emergency."

"So we'll be here a week?"

"Probably. I'll have to install it and then we'll be on our way."

McKenna kneaded Parker's right shoulder. He was right-handed so he'd probably stack to the right, using those muscles more than the others. Parker's moan was more from pleasure than pain.

"I broke protocol today, too." His words were muffled and sleepy sounding.

"How?"

"I'll show you when you're done."

McKenna worked methodically, going from one shoulder to the other and then down his back to his waist. She didn't need to do his legs since most of his muscle use was upper body.

"Do you have any nut allergies?" McKenna asked.

Parker shook his head.

Pouring almond oil into her palms, she applied it liberally to his arms and back. She continued to do so until he fell asleep.

She stood up. Pulling a blanket from his bed, she covered him. Then she got a pillow and slipped it under his head. He stirred a moment, grabbing her hand and tucking it under him. McKenna nearly toppled over. She waited until he settled into a deep sleep, then finger by finger, she slowly extricated it. She'd let him be like that for a while, but he couldn't stay on the floor. With working all day at a job that needed him in good condition, sleeping for hours on the floor was not a good idea.

McKenna plumped the pillows up on her bed and rested against them. She picked up a book she'd been reading. Slipping her finger to the bookmarked section, she opened it and looked at the words. They blurred in front of her. Her eyes went to the man sleeping at the foot of her bed. The blanket rose and fell with his breathing. McKenna caught herself matching her own breathing to the rise and fall of his.

They were so different, she told herself. Yet there were so many qualities and interests they shared. While they might argue at times, they worked together more than against each other. Why else would Parker submit himself to the torture of manual labor for someone he didn't connect with? And she would never have known his true character if she hadn't taken this trip with him. Sometimes their relationship was as rocky and bumpy as the road they traveled, but the road eventually straightened and smoothed.

Parker was Marshall's friend. Was she really doing this for Marshall, she asked herself honestly? Parker had made her remember the truth about this trip. She was enjoying it. Meeting Sherry and Joanna had been pluses in her life, even if she'd only been with them for a short period of time. But day-to-day she was with Parker. He hadn't abandoned her or her quest. She knew there was more to Parker and why he wanted this long drive to California.

"PARKER," MCKENNA WHISPERED an hour later. He didn't stir. She left the bed and got on her knees next to him. Leaning closer, she called his name again. When he didn't open his eyes, she touched his face with the back of one finger. His jaw was slightly coarse with stubble even though he'd shaved that morning. Her hand moved to his hair. It was soft and her fingers threaded through it. "Parker." Her voice was even softer. "Wake up, Parker."

His eyes opened. She was close enough to him to feel the warmth of his breath. He raised his head and his arm went around her.

McKenna bent forward and Parker pulled her closer to him, his mouth seeking hers. Was he awake yet, she wondered? She tried to speak, but his lips closed over hers.

Push him away, her mind told her, but she didn't. Her eyes closed as emotions sailed through her. She let them rage for a second longer, then ended the kiss.

"This is not a dream, Parker."

When she could see he was fully awake and focused, she smiled. He fell back and away from her. She moved away at the same time. Parker drew in a long breath and sat up. Reaching for his shirt, he pulled it on.

"I guess I broke the rules again."

"You were asleep, dreaming." She gave him an excuse, but it was more for her than for him.

He got up and offered her his hand to help her off the floor. McKenna placed her hand in his and he pulled her up. Immediately, she stepped out of embrace territory.

"You're not the only one who broke protocol today," Parker said.

McKenna stared at him. Other than their kiss, what else was newsworthy?"

Parker went to the clothes he'd worn to work. He pulled a couple of papers from a pocket and handed them to her.

"What's this?"

"Look at them."

Unfolding the first paper, she grinned widely. "Where did you get this?" On the page was a picture of Joanna and her parents. They were all smiling and looking like a happy family. Quickly, she opened the second page. It was an email message to Parker's account.

This is us at the lake. My stepfather, Glenn, owns a cabin here and the place has swimming, sailing, horseback riding and everything else you can think of. Plus there's a guy in another cabin with dreamy eyes. I think he notices me. I'll keep you posted.
Joanna

"She's in good spirits," McKenna said as she looked up from the pages. Parker was sitting at the table. "Where did you get these?"

"That's the protocol thing. I got the email

and I printed these in the factory office during my lunch hour. They have a place where you can use a computer. I finished my edits and went to send them in. That's when I saw the message from Joanna."

"Getting the edits done must make you feel good."

"It does, but it's a little scary, too. You never know if they'll come back with more changes."

"Let's hope they don't. Are you going to write another book immediately?"

"I doubt it. Right now I'm making notes on this trip."

"Can I see them?"

"Not yet. When I have some order to them."

McKenna looked down at the papers again. She was a little disappointed. She wanted to know what Parker was writing in relation to her. Probably better not to know, she thought. "I'm so glad things are working out for Joanna."

Parker agreed. His energy level seemed completely restored.

"Did you check all your email?" McKenna asked.

"You'll be proud of me. I spent my remaining time getting to know my coworkers. This is quite a community."

"The part should be here soon and you'll be out of that factory."

"I've developed a huge respect for people who work in factories. Robotics have replaced a lot of people doing repetitive jobs, but for small companies like this one, people still do everything. And they are proud of what they do."

"Sullivan's Travels," she said.

"Who's that? I thought you were Buz and I was Tod?"

McKenna laughed. "It's you. You're Sullivan."

"All right, I'll play along. What's my role now?"

"Sullivan was a rich guy who planned to make a documentary on the plight of Depression-era victims. What he learned during his travels was the power of laughter."

"What you're saying is I started out with one thing in mind, but now it's changed because of what I've learned on the road?"

"I knew you were a quick study," Mc-

Kenna said. "You're not the only one. I've discovered a few things, too."

"Like what?"

"Like…" she hesitated. "Like you're not the stuffy professor I thought you were."

"I know."

"You know I changed my opinion of you?"

He only had to turn those brown eyes and that grin on her for strange things to happen to her insides. Of course, he knew. He'd kissed her just a few minutes ago. Everything that she'd believed about him had wilted under the power of his lips.

ZEKE AND MCKENNA took turns getting lunch. On the fourth day of her working at the garage, it was her turn. She picked up their meals at the restaurant he'd sent her to for coffee that first day. Smiling at the waitress who'd called her Ms. Zeke when she came in wearing his coveralls, she waved as she went out into the bright sunlight. The name began as a joke. It stuck and everyone in the small restaurant referred to her as Ms. Zeke. Secretly, she believed Zeke liked that. He was a widower and he'd taken to her quickly after their initial meeting.

"Lunch," she called as she entered the office. Zeke wasn't there. Lately, he was never there. A steady flow of cars needing attention came in and out of the garage.

She suggested moving the Corvette to free up the bay, but Zeke said they could only work on one at a time and the third bay would be unused anyway.

Zeke came to the door, cleaning his hands. "Mail's here," he said.

McKenna looked up at him. "Is it here?"

"It's got my name on it, but it's from a parts store back east."

McKenna jerked around looking for a package.

"I put it in the bay by the car," Zeke said.

She headed for the door, eager to tear open the box and begin to fix the Corvette.

"Aren't you gonna eat?" he called.

"I'm not hungry," she shouted back.

It wouldn't take her long to install the pump. Maybe she could get it done tonight after she finished working on the car Zeke had assigned her. She could test her work tomorrow and possibly she and Parker would be back on schedule the next day.

She wanted him out of that factory even though he no longer dragged himself home each night. She knew she was the one who felt it more than Parker. He adapted well. While McKenna liked Zeke and she loved the physical work of finding and fixing the problem with cars, she was antsy to keep going. She and Parker had made it almost to the halfway point of their trip. She wanted to go on. She needed to go on. She was getting way too close to Parker for comfort. She couldn't have feelings for Parker. He was the last person on earth she needed to fall for.

Fall for!

McKenna halted her thoughts. She was not falling for Parker. No matter how he made her feel, he was there when Marshall died. She couldn't be in love with him. Yet… she was. She'd fought it, remembered her husband, tried to keep him in her mind when Parker edged him aside. But Parker had unlocked her defenses and taken hold of her heart. Denying it seemed too dishonest now.

McKenna ripped the box with the water

pump in it harder than she'd expected. It was the correct model. All the gaskets, glue and other parts were inside. A rush of adrenaline made her want to begin the repair immediately. The sooner she got the Corvette back on the road, the sooner she could return to her former life.

Why didn't thoughts of that make her happy? They seemed to have the opposite effect instead.

"McKenna, why don't I finish the engine block on the Camaro?" Zeke proposed. "I know you want to get to this right away."

Misty emotion filled her eyes. She came just short of flying across the floor and straight into his arms.

"I'm gonna hate losing my lady mechanic, but I knew it had to happen someday."

This time she did hug him. "Thank you, Zeke."

McKenna went right to work and in just a couple of hours, the car was ready to test. She went in search of Zeke.

He was pumping gas. She saw him through the office window, where her un-eaten lunch still sat. Her stomach growled at the thought of the food. She left and cleaned her hands, then came back and dove into her sandwich and watery drink.

"Finished?" Zeke asked coming into the office.

"All done," she said between bites. "It's ready to test."

Zeke glanced toward the wall. The Corvette couldn't be seen from here.

"Why don't you go test it?" McKenna suggested.

She watched a series of expressions cross his craggy face.

"You don't mean that?" he said.

"Ever drive a Corvette?"

"Been one of my dreams since I got my first Hot Wheels car at age three."

"It wasn't a Studebaker?"

Zeke laughed. "I got that one at age four."

"Go on," she said. "The keys are in it."

Zeke took off like a man finding his dream. She heard the motor start and walked outside to see the Corvette back out of the garage. Heading for the highway, he waved his hat in the air like a cowboy as he let out a loud yell. McKenna smiled as he peeled down the main street.

"DID YOU ENJOY your stay?" Parker asked as he angled the car out of Catoosa.

"I did. Zeke offered me a job if I ever need one." She laughed. "I guess I'll always think of him working on his Studebaker."

Parker had seen the car in the garage. "That's his?"

She nodded. "He's been working on restoring it for months. It needs an engine before he can go any further."

"Think he can find one or will he have to build it?"

"He has sources, auto clubs, classic car dealers. Still, he'll probably have to build it. What about you? Are you glad to be on the road again?"

"Being at the factory was an experience I wouldn't want to repeat any time soon. My back still aches. But it served its purpose and, like I said, I definitely have a new respect for people who live that life and make mine easier."

The road changed outside Catoosa, transforming from smooth blacktop to cracked pavement to hard concrete and back to smooth blacktop. Parker wished they were on the highway. He wanted to drive fast and get where they were going.

Since arriving in Catoosa, his relationship with McKenna had been hot and cold. Right now they were on a warm setting, but sparks could flare up at any moment, either good ones or bad ones. He was sure they were headed for an explosion and he wanted to get to their destination first to try to ward it off.

Maybe she felt the same, since they drove farther and for longer than they had since leaving Chicago. They crossed Oklahoma and the Texas Panhandle, taking time to stop at the Cadillac Ranch for some photos before it was on to Santa Fe and stopping for the night. They found a motel and dinner, during which they didn't talk much.

"New Mexico is a beautiful state," Parker said, wanting to break the silence. "We missed a lot of it after the sunset."

"You've been here before?"

"Many times. I've been to conferences and art shows."

"Art shows? You like southwestern art?"

"I appreciate some of it. It was Loretta who was the true lover of art. She'd come with me if I had a meeting out here. When we parted, her collection of silver and turquoise was quite extensive." Parker noticed McKenna's eyes opened slightly wider with the mention of his ex-wife's name. It was the first time he'd mentioned her without being prompted. "I have a couple of landscape paintings I bought there."

"Did the artist become famous?"

"I never checked. They hang in my office. Maybe you'd like to see them when we get back."

It was an invitation for her to visit him. Parker hadn't thought of that when he made the statement. But he wasn't about to take the words back and he didn't regret them. He could picture her standing in his office, viewing the paintings.

One reflected the colors of the land and buildings, the sandy mountains in the background. Parker was drawn to it by its sparseness. The painting and the land needed nothing more and the artist had captured that. The second painting was of desert flowers. Again sparse pops of green on an adobe-colored background and one white bud looking as if it was fighting to survive among the harsh sun and waterless terrain.

"I would," McKenna said.

Parker had only a second to look at her in the moving car, but their eyes met and he saw something there. He had to focus on the road, but he was sure McKenna had masked her feelings as soon as she thought he could see them.

At that moment he made a decision. There was something he had to do. She wasn't going to like it, but he was going to do it anyway. He had to find out the truth.

"WE SEEM TO be rushing," McKenna said the next day when Parker took over the driving at a rest area. They'd left New Mexico behind and were heading for Arizona. "We've only stopped long enough for me to take a few pictures."

"Is there someplace particular you'd like to stop?" Parker asked. "There isn't much to see along this stretch of road."

"It isn't that. I guess it's that the end of the trip is in sight. We've been on the road for over a month. And we only have one more state to cross. Maybe I'm feeling restless because we're getting on each other's nerves."

"Am I getting on your nerves?" Parker asked. "You're not getting on mine."

"Not even with all my stubbornness? Not with having to share your space with me, not to mention being in a car that only holds two people and the space between us is teeny-tiny?"

"You're very refreshing, McKenna," he laughed. "You have no idea the effect you have on people."

"What effect?"

"Mostly, that they like you. Right away you win them over. They always trust you. And you tend to make them feel comfortable instead of pushing your brain on them."

"My brain?" she said with a frown.

"That's what I mean. You're not even aware you're doing it."

"Doing what?" she asked.

"You're one of the most intelligent people I have ever met, yet when people assume you know nothing, you don't get angry or righteous, you just prove how smart you are and you never make them feel belittled. It's a quality I love." Parker shot a glance her way. He wondered if she'd pick up on the last word or if she'd assume it was only a figure of speech.

"That's a nice thing to say. I want people to treat me the way I treat them. For the most part they do."

"Who taught you to act that way? I know your parents died when you were young. Who brought you up?"

"My parents died when I was a senior in college. The person I relied on after that was Marshall. My mom and dad were honest, fun-loving people. They did a lot of things together and I never remember either one of them making malicious fun of the other. Maybe I've inherited the characteristic."

Parker envied her. Even though her parents were gone, they'd left her a legacy that would get her ahead. Parker knew people responded positively to her.

His parents had been quite different from hers. His father was stern, approving of nothing and no one. When Parker wanted to go to college, he chose schools that were far from home. His father refused to pay. Belligerent at the time, Parker walked away without a nickel of support. Or any of the emotional kind, either.

It was hard work and a stroke of luck that he got a full scholarship and met some good people, including Marshall. After graduation and his post-doc work, he landed a college teaching job and thought that was how he'd spend the rest of his life.

"Did you reconcile with your parents?" McKenna asked.

"How did you know we weren't the model family?" She always surprised him with her insight.

"You told me about the backyard campout that didn't happen. Your sister is in China and your brother is in Washington State. Your tone when you mentioned him wasn't a happy one. And since then you haven't brought them up in conversation. I figured there must be something that keeps you from talking about them."

"My mother is wonderful. How she managed to marry a man as domineering as my father is a mystery to me. He loves her completely. I have no doubt of that, but I never knew who I or my sister and brother were to him."

"How's your relationship now?"

"We tolerate each other at holidays, weddings and funerals."

"That's not much of a relationship," McKenna said.

"No, I suppose it isn't."

"Parker, you don't realize how lucky you are to have parents. I'd give…" She stopped then and he saw the emotion on her face, even though she was staring straight ahead through the windshield.

"You're a different type of person because of what you went through," he told her.

"You'll regret not having a better relationship with him in the future."

"I don't think so," Parker replied.

"Take my word for it. Like you recognized Joanna as a runaway, I know you'll miss your parents when they're gone. You still have the opportunity to change that. You should take it."

"What should I do? I can't force my father to love me."

"You don't think he loves you?" McKenna asked.

"In his own way, perhaps."

"So you're punishing your mother because you don't want to approach your father."

"I see her..."

"Yes, on holidays, weddings and funerals. How often do they happen?"

"MY FATHER DOESN'T want to see me. I couldn't wait to get out of my parents' house. The ironic thing is, I now support them and my father has never even said he's appreciated the help."

"Is that the way you see it?"

"See what?" Parker asked.

"That he needs to come to you and say thank-you for the help."

"It would be nice."

"It wouldn't."

"McKenna, I have no idea how you're coming up with these assumptions when you hardly know a thing about my relationship with my parents."

She considered how harsh his tone was. He obviously didn't want to discuss his parents. Yes, he missed his mother, but he and his father had never looked at the same thing with a compatible eye.

"I know I should drop the subject. It's obviously uncomfortable for you, but as someone who has so much insight into other people, you're extremely blinded by your own situation."

"Can we drop this subject?"

"Sure we can, but that doesn't mean you won't keep thinking about it. What you'll do is suppress it, force it to the back of your mind until something else covers it over and you don't have to deal with it. All that does is postpone the inevitable. It creates a bomb that will eventually explode over something unrelated to the real reason."

"I suppose this is what happened to you?"

"Yes," she whispered in a voice that wouldn't allow Parker to explore it. If he didn't want her probing into his family history, he shouldn't be allowed to delve into hers.

"When my parents passed away, I never cried. I went through the ritual of the funeral. I listened to all the platitudes and said all the right things. Whenever anyone mentioned them, I'd change the subject, make a joke, or find a reason to leave the room. It was Marshall who understood what I was doing. He explained what would happen if I didn't let go of the emotions I was holding inside. I didn't believe it. I didn't even accept that he was right. In my mind I was fine."

"What happened?"

"I exploded, not over anything having to do with my parents. It was a coffee cup in a restaurant."

"A cup?"

"I was having lunch about a year after their deaths. The waitress served my coffee in a cup that had a trace of someone's lipstick on the edge of it. Instead of asking for a clean cup, I ranted at her, totally lost my cool. I called her stupid, and asked if she understood her job. I went on and on like a crazy woman. I was crazy. With pent-up emotion. And once I'd started, I couldn't stop. I could see myself acting completely out of character, but I couldn't stop."

"What did the waitress do?"

"I don't know. Marshall heard the commotion. He rushed in, dropped some money on the table and carried me out of there. I cried it out in his arms."

"You don't expect me to cry it out?"

"I have no right to expect anything of you. I can only tell you that if you don't resolve issues when you can, they'll change you as a human being."

"So I'll end up a lonely old man with nothing to show for my life and no one to mourn my death."

She looked straight at him as if his prediction was how it was going to be. But she knew better. He'd have plenty to show for his life and as far as having no one to mourn him, he couldn't be more wrong.

CHAPTER THIRTEEN

THE REST OF the drive to Flagstaff was in silence. McKenna didn't regret what she'd said, but the timing and how she said them could have been better.

Parker was obviously thinking about what she'd said. His brow was furrowed as if he were looking into the sun.

It was noon when they arrived in Arizona. Stopping at rest areas along the way, McKenna picked up magazines and brochures offering discounts at motels and hotels.

"There's a motel that seems to be clean and cheap enough for us," she told Parker. He didn't appear to be listening to her. In fact, instead of turning toward the center of town, he turned the opposite way.

"There's someplace I want to go," Parker said.

"A detour?" After their conversation yesterday, McKenna thought it best to let him lead the discussion.

After a while, he turned the car onto US Route 180, going north. Parker drove the road as if he was familiar with it. He seemed to know exactly where he was going and had been there many times before.

"What's our destination here?" McKenna finally had to ask after they'd been driving about ten minutes.

"To a little mountain resort about fifteen miles from here. We'll stay there for the night."

"A resort. Can we afford it?"

"This is summer, so the rates are a lot lower than they would be in winter."

She stiffened as if making the connection to the reason for this detour. "Why are we going there?

"Marshall." His one word was clipped and succinct.

The last fifteen miles to the resort were met with increasing tension. McKenna wondered if she was about to eat her own words. She'd lectured Parker about ridding himself of pent-up emotions. Was that what he was doing for her? Was he taking her to the place where Marshall died?

The resort was a log cabin–looking building that was the size of a mansion. The lobby was lined with dark wood. A huge stone fireplace covered a far wall. Comfortable chairs were placed together and arranged around the room. A stairway led to an upper floor where she could see doors to the rooms.

Parker checked them in and the desk clerk said there was an elevator that led to the third floor. Parker reached for her and with his hand on her lower back, guided her to the elevator. He didn't stumble or make a misstep. He knew this building's layout.

"You must have stayed here with Marshall and the others," she stated.

"Eight of us in total. We were on the second floor. The one that overlooks the lobby."

"I remember he liked to ski in Arizona, but I didn't know it was here. I thought it was one of the other, more popular areas."

Marshall belonged to a ski club and loved the sport. The group made a minimum of two trips a season.

"This one's quieter. Less traffic on the slopes," Parker said.

After the charged atmosphere of Chicago, Marshall would love a slower pace. McKenna liked that, too. She could see herself sitting before a fire in the lobby, enjoying a glass of wine after a long day. However, skiing was not something she enjoyed. She'd done it three times and had never gone back to it. That was why she wasn't with Marshall when he died.

DROPPING THEIR BACKPACKS on the beds, Parker immediately led McKenna out of the room. They walked back to the car and Parker drove them a short distance away and up a steep road.

"What are we doing here?" she asked. McKenna looked around. There was nothing there. No one else was in the parking lot except them.

Parker pulled the car into a space and cut the engine. He got out and came around to the passenger side. Opening the door, he offered McKenna his hand. She looked at it as if debating whether to accept his offer. Then she put her hand in his and he gently pulled her to her feet.

Her hand was soft. He hadn't touched her in a while and the contact had the predictable effect on him, warm, protective and loving.

"Parker, why are we here?"

"This is the real reason for your trip."

The air was crisp and clean. The sky a perfect blue. A slight breeze disturbed her hair. He wanted to catch it and push his fingers through it.

"What real reason?" she asked.

"This is where it happened, McKenna."

He watched her jaw tighten. Her body became stiff and she looked across the lot at the mountain in the distance.

"There's nothing here. This is a scenic overview where motorists could pull off the mountain and take pictures before continuing their journey. What would Marshall be doing here?"

"Not here in the parking lot. Up there." He pointed to the top of the mountain.

"How high is that?"

"Over 11,500 feet."

"That's within range." Marshall had sickle cell trait. He couldn't fly without oxygen. Going higher than 14,000 feet while doing a physical activity could cause him to dehydrate and become so tired as to go into crisis, but 11,500 was within the safety zone.

"Only if Marshall was in tip-top condition. Which he wasn't. And that wasn't all."

"Why didn't you stop him?" McKenna asked. "You knew his condition. You were his friend. How could you let him take that run?"

Her voice was a mere whisper. The breeze about them made more noise. She seemed too angry to shout.

"McKenna, Marshall's been dead for three years. I have the feeling you've never read the police report, never looked at his death certificate."

She dropped her head. "I knew he had sickle cell trait."

"Do you have it, too?" It was a long shot, but Parker asked, anyway.

She stalked away from him then. "I had the doctors test me when Marshall told me he had it. I wanted to have children, and needed to know if they would possibly have the disease. And then he was gone." Her voice cracked on the last word.

"Marshall didn't die from sickle cell trait. He had something else. Something we never knew about until after the fact. If he knew about it, he kept it from all of us."

McKenna turned and looked at him.

"Sit down," Parker said.

McKenna headed for a visitors, bench nearby. It faced the mountain where people could take in the scenic beauty of the landscape. The ski trails were on the other side, out of direct view. Parker sat next to her.

"The coroner discovered that Marshall had a disease called AMS, acute mountain sickness. It's rare and often associated with another disease called high-altitude cerebral edema. Together these conditions have serious drawbacks. However, a skier is relatively safe under 14,000 feet."

"We're under 14,000."

Parker paused, allowing McKenna to process what he was telling her. "The cerebral edema condition and the sickle cell combined, causing him to become drowsy, confused and disoriented. He passed out. Search and rescue didn't find him for over an hour. By then it was too late."

"Where were you?" she asked.

Parker knew that was coming and was prepared for it. He would tell her now, looking her directly in the face. "The group of us had left the slope to get ready for dinner. Marshall said he'd forgotten something at the lift and would be right in. I went to my room. He must have decided to take one more run before coming back."

"What did he forget?" Unshed tears made her eyes glisten, he noticed.

Parker stood up and reached into his pocket. He drew out a small medallion on a broken chain. McKenna rose from the bench and took it.

"Why would he leave this behind?"

"He realized the chain had broken just as we were getting on the ski lift. We had our gloves and poles, everything on. It was awkward to unzip a pocket. Marshall asked the lift operator to hold it for him. He'd come back to get it after our run."

McKenna stared down at the golden disk.

"I gave him this," she said. She rubbed her thumb over the raised engraving of a car. On the back were their initials entwined. "The car represented the first one we owned together. I had two of these medallions made. I didn't know Marshall had his with him. After he died, I never looked for it. When they sent his effects, I never went through them."

"This one was sent to me." Parker's heart thudded hard against his chest when she looked up at him.

Their faces close, maybe too close.

"The lift operator forgot Marshall's name, but he remembered mine. The note he sent said he'd forgotten all about it, having put it in his pocket at the end of that day. As the season was finishing, he hadn't worn those same clothes again until he sent them to be cleaned. The cleaners returned the chain and pendant to him and he got my address from the clerk and sent them to me to pass on."

"Thank you," McKenna said. She closed her fingers slowly over the medallion.

Parker took a deep breath. This would make or break whether he and McKenna would ever be anything but friends. "I brought you here for two reasons," he said.

"What are they?" Again, the softness of her voice was nearly his undoing.

"I wanted to tell you the whole truth. I know you blamed me for Marshall's death."

"Can you ever forgive me?" McKenna asked. "I am so, so sorry. I thought since the two of you were such good friends, you could have and should have done something to prevent it happening. But you weren't there. It wasn't your fault."

"And I'm sure," he told her. "I'm sure Marshall didn't know about the AMS. The group of us had come here before, but never when that trail was open. Usually we stayed at the lower elevations. This time it seemed the snow was right and the trail was open. And the elevation was within the safety limit."

"But for a broken chain..." she said.

"Let's go back," McKenna said.

"Back to the hotel or back to Flagstaff?"

"The hotel," she clarified. "We've driven a long while today and a lot of weight has been lifted from both our shoulders. But even though the load is lighter, I'm still tired. I'm betting you are, too."

They returned to the car and Parker opened the passenger side door for her. Before getting in the Corvette, McKenna put her hands on his shoulders and kissed his cheek.

He seemed to search her eyes for a long moment. So long that the tension between them stirred again. McKenna wondered what he was thinking. His head dipped forward and she caught her breath.

Stopping him from completing his intended action, she spoke. "You said there were two reasons you brought me here. What's the second one?"

"To say goodbye, if you want to. You never have."

McKenna peered over his shoulder at the mountain that had taken her husband. She no longer felt the sharp pain of loss. She felt renewed, ready to go on and begin once more.

"Goodbye, Marshall," she whispered. "I'm going to be all right." She addressed the wind as she took Parker's arm and raised her gaze to meet his.

Standing face to face, she moved her arms to his neck and pulled his mouth to hers. Immediately Parker crushed her to him, kissing her long and hard, wanting to continue holding her until the sun set and rose again.

IT WAS AS IF that soft breeze on the mountain blew away years of mistrust. The air between her and Parker was so clean.

McKenna woke in the resort bed. A sliver of light peeked through the curtains telling her she'd slept longer than usual. Maybe because when she'd gone to bed she and Parker were friends. Friends who'd kissed a couple of times, but were not lovers. She could no longer make him her enemy or blame him for her husband's death.

Parker had told her going to the mountain was her real reason for taking this trip. She admitted that could have been true. Although she'd had no intention of going there at all, she'd recognized she would be near the place as she drove on Route 66. Maybe she'd have made the detour alone. She'd never know.

Actually seeing the mountain was better than imagining what it looked like. And finding that out, knowing the truth released her from the bonds that had held her immobile for three years, felt good. Life was brighter this morning than it had ever been in the past three years. She had a new energy and was ready for the next adventure.

Something else had occurred to her. That her seeing the place where Marshall died was also Parker's reason for insisting on accompanying her. When she thought back over their small arguments about returning to Chicago, he'd given in rather quickly. He never wanted to go back. He wanted to get to this place so he could show her the mountain and tell her the truth.

It was worth it, she thought.

Getting up, she went to the bathroom, washed and dressed. Parker was waiting when she came out. They smiled as they passed each other.

"Ready for breakfast?" he asked when he emerged from the bathroom ten minutes later, his hair still wet from a morning shower. She remembered the feel of his hair in Catoosa when he'd fallen asleep on the floor in their room.

"Ready," she said. McKenna drove them to a nearby restaurant where they had great food and coffee for less than half the price of the resort breakfast. "I picked up some brochures in the lobby on skydiving in Phoenix." She pulled them out of her purse and laid them on the table.

"You're still interested in doing that?" he practically blurted.

"Of course. I've done some of the things I always wanted to do. You should, too. This might be your only chance to do them." McKenna regretted the words as soon as she said them.

"Don't do that," Parker said.

"Do what?"

"Don't edit yourself like that. Everything doesn't apply to Marshall's untimely death. There are going to be comments that can be taken both ways, but only if you mean them as such. And I'll know if that's the case."

"All right." She plucked up a brochure.

"I've been checking our finances again. This is expensive. We'll need jobs in order to do this and get to California."

"I hope to find something that doesn't involve boxes and shipping." He laughed. It was the first time McKenna truly appreciated hearing it.

PHOENIX WAS ANOTHER detour off Route 66. Driving into the flat countryside of adobe houses and a bustling downtown core was like finding a smaller version of Chicago set among a moonscape. Cacti surprised them, growing in unexpected places, as did seeing homes with airplane hangars in place of garages.

McKenna got her camera out and began snapping pictures.

"You must have quite a photo history of this trip," Parker said.

"I do. I'm going to bore Adrienne, Lydia and Sara to death when we get back."

"We are getting close to the end," he said. "Glad you came?"

"I've loved this. I am so glad I had the courage to do it."

"Courage, you? I never doubted for a minute that you were afraid of anything."

"Not afraid, exactly," McKenna said. "At least not until my friends made me doubt myself. Their intentions were good, but I'm glad I ignored their advice. Given everything that's happened so far, I wouldn't have missed this for the world."

"Even the robbery?" he asked, his eyes crinkling at the edges.

"Okay. Not that, but if it hadn't been for the robbery, we might not have met Joanna and Sherry. I wouldn't be Ms. Zeke. And you and I could still be polite enemies."

"Then it was worth every mile, every muscle ache, every bad meal and hard bed."

McKenna smiled.

"Look," Parker said. "There's a help-wanted sign. Here's a place where I know my way around."

He waited at a light and made a left turn onto a road that led to the University of Phoenix campus. Following the road where it led, he eventually stopped at not one but three buildings before locating the right spot. McKenna waited in the car until he returned.

The job was janitorial. They needed an extra cleaner for the classroom buildings. He'd work nights from six till ten. It paid union scale, which was more than minimum wage, and he didn't have to be a member of the union.

"The job is temporary," the hiring manager had told Parker. "We got a guy on medical leave. He could be back in a week, maybe six weeks. Not sure when. You know, insurance companies run the hospitals and doctors' offices now."

"Not a problem. I'll only be here a few weeks at the most," Parker replied honestly. "I can help out until he returns or you hire someone permanently."

"There's a lot of paperwork to fill out, even for temporary employees. This is a school, so we have to be careful of people with arrest records..."

"Sexual predators, child molesters, I know the drill," Parker finished for him. "Tell me where to go and I'll start completing those forms."

They'd shaken hands and Parker headed for the administration building.

JOBS DIDN'T DROP in McKenna's lap the same way they appeared to do with Parker. He'd barely step on the ground when a job would be right there waiting for him. She had to go from place to place, searching for something, anything.

This time, she decided to cut her losses by starting with a temporary agency. Willing to do either one-day assignments or work at the same place for a small amount of time got her steady work.

As they sat at breakfast later, Parker took a drink of his coffee and set the cup down. "I know you always do the finances, but by my calculations, it will take two weeks for both of us to get a paycheck. That would cover the cost of skydiving if we didn't have expenses like eating and lodging.

"In order to pay for everything and live, we're going to have to do something else."

"Any ideas?" she asked.

"One. Our greatest outlay of cash is the motel. I spoke with the university and asked if we could somehow stay on campus, given it's the summer session."

"On campus? You mean like in a dorm room?" McKenna smiled. She wasn't opposed to dorms. It had been years.

"Don't jump so quickly, there's a catch." He wagged a finger at her, grinning.

"What is it?"

"Since I have a connection with a university they are willing to accept my credentials and allow me to have a room."

"And me?"

"The room is for married students."

"We're not married."

"I didn't tell them that."

McKenna didn't know how to respond. "We need to pretend to be married? What if it's for a while, not just a week or so?" She mentally did the math, figuring out how much money they would need for skydiving and living expenses, plus they still needed to pay for gas to get to California.

"People have been thinking we were married all the while as we've driving across country. This time we'll just not tell them the complete truth."

"You mean I should lie?" she asked.

"I mean you should focus on reaching a goal. If it would hurt someone, I'd say no. But there seems to be no harm here and we'll get to California that much faster."

Parker's logic wasn't flawless, but it was reasonable. The alternative would be to eliminate the skydiving and just go on to California, but it was the only thing he'd said he really wanted to do. So far McKenna had done what she'd set out to do. Parker should have a chance to do the same and she wanted to be the one to help him do it. He'd more than earned this one reward.

"Okay," she said. "If you can stand me as your wife, even temporarily, I can do it."

"You're not the Wicked Witch of the West," he said.

"No, I'm from the East."

PARKER THOUGHT THE university housing was a stroke of luck, especially since he and McKenna were traveling so light they had their backpacks in the car and could check out of the motel without returning.

After work that evening, the true light of

their decision presented itself as the two of them stood in the doorway of a married-students dorm room. There were no cooking facilities, although there was a mini refrigerator in the corner. It had a sign on it proclaiming it Property of the University of Phoenix.

In the center of the room was a double bed, unmade, but with two sheets and a blanket folded and waiting.

McKenna stepped inside. Parker closed the door and they both stared at the one bed.

"Any suggestions?" she asked.

He looked at her. "I'll take the floor."

"You can't sleep on the floor," she told him. "Doing that will make your back ache. And someone planning to go skydiving doesn't need to begin the adventure with a disadvantage."

Looking around the room, Parker saw two doors. He assumed they were closets. One led to a small bathroom containing a shower, no tub. The other however led to a small sitting room. "There's a sofa!" he exclaimed as if he'd discovered the cure for the common cold.

McKenna followed after him. The room was tiny, but it contained a flat screen television, a sofa, a table and chairs for studying.

"I'll take this," she said. "I'm shorter." She went over and sat on the sofa. It was hard. She lay down, tucking her arm under her head. "It's perfect."

And so their routine began as a married couple.

CHAPTER FOURTEEN

THE YOUNG MAN couldn't be more than nineteen. This was probably the summer after his freshman year at the university, judging by the textbook he dropped on the classroom floor. Parker read the white letters on a muted green background—Introduction to Economics.

The man looked up at him as if he'd been caught doing something wrong. His teenage acne was clearing up. By the time he reached Parker's age, he wouldn't remember the angst of this period in his life.

"Sorry," he said. "I didn't think anyone was here." He started to rise.

"Stay." Parker put his hand out to stop him. "You're not in my way."

The man gave him a shy smile and resumed his seat. He opened the book about a third of the way in.

"Summer school?" Parker asked, opening a conversation, while he pushed the large broom around gathering the remnants of a day's debris.

He winced. "And this course is kicking my butt. I probably would do better if I'd studied Greek, since this seems like a foreign language to me."

Parker stifled a laugh. "It can't be that bad. It's just a few graphs."

"That's just it, it's all graphs. Some don't make sense to me. Most of them don't make sense."

"What's your major?" Parker asked.

"I haven't declared one, but believe me, it won't be Economics." The man glanced with disgust at the open textbook.

Parker leaned his broom against the doorway and approached the young man. He perched on a desk next to him.

"Parker Fordum," he said, offering his hand.

The young man took it and shook firmly. "Austin Rockwell."

"Well, Austin, let's look at what you need to do."

"You know this stuff?" Austin asked, surprise evident in his voice.

"I've taken a course or two." Parker didn't want to intimidate him by telling him he taught the subject and that he'd written the textbook he was using. The young man would learn more if he thought the two of them were on an even footing.

Parker took the book. "This is the first course in Econ," he said.

Austin nodded.

"The initial course is designed to give you a taste of the entire field of economics."

Austin nodded.

"After this there are other courses that will deal with only a single portion of what's in this book."

"Well, I don't plan to enroll in any more."

Parker laughed. "I felt the same way when I took my first course."

"But you went for more?" The young man questioned his sanity.

Parker smiled. "I did. After a while I became interested specifically in the way money worked and how it could be analyzed."

"This isn't money," Austin said. "I mean it isn't real money."

"Oh, believe me, it's real."

Parker saw the young man frown.

"There are micro and macro principles involved, currency issues and things like GDP, which involve huge sums, and the means by which it all changes hands is complex and fascinating. Even things like a loan through a bank are tied up in it, too. And small amounts, like when Americans go to a foreign country and spend their dollars or foreigners come here and do the same. Then there's the stock market, that's definitely about real money."

Austin leaned back in his chair. "You know a lot about this?"

Parker smiled.

"So why are you pushing a broom on a Friday night instead of drinking an expensive wine at a faculty party?"

Parker tipped his head back and chuckled. "It's about the money," he said. "I'm on an adventure and working part-time."

"So your real job is an economist?"

Parker thought a moment. "You could say

that. I'm a professor at the University of Chicago."

"No way," he scoffed, slouching back in his chair and crossing his arms. "Wait a minute. If you're an economist, you should be rolling in dough and not need to be a part-time janitor."

"Now, that's a long story and for another time. Why don't we concentrate on your studies right now?"

McKENNA LISTENED FROM the doorway. She'd never seen Parker teach before. His technique was flawless. Lydia had said Parker's students loved him, that his office hours were generally standing room only. At the time she'd wondered if it was all women waiting for some face time with a handsome professor. But now she understood his appeal.

He'd put the student at ease, got him to talk about his problem and then offered to help him with it. She learned more about Parker every day.

The two men stood at the blackboard. It looked nothing like McKenna remembered when she was in school. It was covered in charts and graphs and they were deep in conversation. McKenna didn't want to interrupt. They were engrossed, but she had the only car and their motel was too far away for Parker to walk. Slipping inside unnoticed, she took a seat near the door. Remaining quiet, she studied them while they talked for ten more minutes before the younger man saw her.

Parker turned around. "McKenna, I didn't know you were there."

"You two were so involved, I didn't want to disturb you."

Parker glanced at the young man. "This is Austin. He's having trouble with his economics class. I was giving him a few pointers."

"Hello," McKenna said.

Austin nodded acknowledgment. "It was more than a few pointers. The way he explains things, it's easy to understand. Almost fun."

"Good to hear," Parker said. "We won't be long," he told McKenna.

"That's all right," Austin said. "We're done." He looked at Parker. "Thank you very much. I have a better understanding of it now." He offered his hand and the two shook.

"How about we meet here on Monday, same time?" Parker's eyebrows rose in question. "I'm willing to help you as long as I'm here."

"I don't want to impose."

"It's up to you. I'll be here regardless."

"Then I'll see you Monday." He smiled and gathered his books. "Nice to meet you," he said to McKenna before leaving them alone.

"He seemed very satisfied."

Parker retrieved the broom and went back to sweeping the floor. "He's a nice kid. Just needed a little direction."

"You were wonderful," McKenna said.

Parker stopped and faced her.

"I've never seen you teaching before. You were so…" She was lost for a description. "So you," she finished.

"What does that mean?"

"You were passionate about it. I could see it."

"You don't think I'm passionate about anything?"

McKenna knew she'd touched a nerve. Why didn't she think before she spoke? "I didn't mean that the way it sounded."

"Just how did you mean it?"

She stood up, feeling at a disadvantage sitting in the small desk. "I meant that you don't show your feelings. You hide everything inside. This was the first time I've seen you in a situation where your love of something comes through. You obviously love teaching."

He stared at her for a moment, but then his shoulders dropped. McKenna let out a slow breath.

"You don't know me, McKenna. There are many things I'm passionate about." He ended the sentence there and returned to sweeping. She knew a door had closed between them just then. It was her fault, but she didn't understand why. What had she said or done that was so wrong? She might have bungled her words, but she meant no insult.

It seemed with Parker, she could never stay on the same level. One day they were friends and suddenly they were not. Or she couldn't figure out what the problem was between them.

"Can I help?" she asked softly.

He sighed. "You can erase the board."

McKenna moved to the board and picked up an eraser. Instantly she was back in grade school, when erasing the blackboard was an honor. The smell of chalk hadn't changed even in this digital age.

"I meant it, Parker," she said as she started removing Parker's handwriting from the second board. This one was full of graphs with notations along the sides.

"Meant what?"

"I meant it when I said you were a wonderful teacher. I could tell by the way the two of you were so into discussing the gross national product."

"Thank you," he said. McKenna noted the deepness of his voice. He was touched by her comment, but like his usual behavior, he held it inside.

DENYING THAT HE had cold feet about jumping from an airplane and falling through the sky would be a lie on Parker's part. He wanted to go skydiving. He'd been thinking about it for a month. Ever since McKenna asked him what he most wanted to do and since their drive into Phoenix, he'd wanted to see what it was like to free-fall. Now the day was here, but Parker was unsure if he was ready for it.

The jump would be a tandem jump. He would be with an experienced jumper, not alone between the sky and the earth. Yet fear and sweat vied against the control he was clinging on to. McKenna had saved every penny she made that wasn't spent on food for them. At some of her temp jobs, they even provided breakfast for the employees.

One job took her to the US Airways Arena where the Phoenix Suns played basketball. As a perk, they'd given her a blanket with the team logo on it. She used it to sleep under on the sofa.

Parker marveled at how she could remain steady on the course she'd set. It was months now since they'd left Chicago and she'd done whatever was necessary to keep going, even to the point of playing the role of his wife—in name only, he added. Most people with her ability and access to her income and lifestyle would have given up this idea and returned to the soft cushion of their former existence. But not McKenna Wellington. She was soldiering onward. Parker loved that about her. In fact, he loved her. He'd always loved her. But only he knew it.

They reached the airport at noon. Parker refused to eat any lunch before the jump.

"Scared?" she asked as they got out of the car and headed for the plane.

"If I said yes, would you think less of me?"

"If you lied, I'd think less of you."

"All right, I'm scared."

"You took the course. You know what to do."

"Theory and practice are separate and sometimes unequal things."

McKenna laughed at his sarcasm. She took his arm and stopped him. Looking at him, her expression serious, she said. "I won't think any less of you if you don't want to go through with this." She looked as if she was a little scared, too.

Parker pecked her on the cheek. "I really want to do this."

Thirty minutes later he was in the plane, strapped to a stranger as if he were a giant baby and McKenna was on the ground, waiting. Then he was out the door and the ground was coming toward him fast. McKenna had insisted on including a second parachutist to make a recording of the jump. Parker was petrified until the parachute opened.

Once the parachute deployed, he was floating and had the chance to really look at the scenery, marvel in the beauty of the earth until his tandem partner took control of a soft landing.

"What a rush," Parker shouted as he reached McKenna. Someone had come and unhooked his harness, allowing him to walk, abeit on shaky legs.

"Did you like it?" she asked.

"It was the best thing I've ever done. I loved it!" Excitement tinged his words and Parker gathered McKenna in a great big hug. He was over-animated and he knew it, but he couldn't help himself. He felt like a little boy again, enthusiastic in discovering the world and how much there was to see and do. He tended to be conservative, but that personality trait was totally forgotten in light of a fall to the earth.

"You have got to try this," he said, swinging McKenna around. "Thank you for talking me into it. I couldn't have done it without you."

"I see it's going to take a while for you to calm down," she said. "Don't you think you should put me back on the ground? You're the one who was airborne."

He set her down as if he'd forgotten he was holding her.

"I don't think I'll ever calm down. I was scared to go up, really scared. But this was the best, incomparable."

McKenna listened to him patiently for the entire drive back to the dorm. He had the video of the jump and couldn't resist playing it on his computer. McKenna watched the less than five minute feature with him and oohed and ahhed in all the right spots.

"I wish you'd been up there with me. It was just the best experience."

"Maybe one day," McKenna said.

He went on telling her about his experience until darkness fell and she was clearly exhausted. It was as if skydiving had opened a door for him and he couldn't close it.

"I guess today was worth all the previous

days of working, pain and unexpected experiences," she said.

Parker sobered. "I wouldn't miss any one of those days, if given the choice. And if I had to do them over, I'd do it without complaint."

He didn't smile or give her any indication that he was anything but genuine. He could see the fright in her eyes and the small movement of a vein in her throat that told him her heartbeat had increased.

"It's a shame we have to follow up a day like today with our jobs tomorrow," she said.

Parker nodded. "I'll let you go to sleep."

He rose and started for the bedroom. Once inside, he quietly closed the door. He didn't want to leave her. He wanted to stay and talk. He wanted to sit on the sofa, holding her to him, slipping his fingers through her hair. He wanted to tell her he loved her.

It had been a wonderful day. Still, he wanted more.

THE NEXT MORNING they drove the final four hundred miles to the Pacific Coast Highway in Santa Monica. The Pacific Ocean welcomed them with soft waves and sounds that were like relaxing music to their ears. McKenna stood next to a large rock and smelled the salt and sea. Parker came up beside her.

"We made it," she said.

"With only a few mishaps."

"Those were adventures." She grinned, correcting him. "I had a wonderful time. I'm sorry it has to end. The car's running like a dream, as smoothly as if it was being serviced by a professional pit crew. I feel like it could go another 3,000 miles easy before we'd need to stop again."

"I'm sorry to see the trip end, too," Parker said, sounding sincere. "But we knew we had to get to this day."

McKenna inhaled a deep breath and released it. "It seems like it was only a few days ago I was arguing with you in my driveway."

He squatted down, picking up a couple of pebbles and stared at the water. "I did it, McKenna."

"Did what? Are you back to skydiving again?"

"I called my father. It was after the skydiving. You went to sleep. I went to my room and I contacted him. We talked for several hours. You were right. We did need to sort things out between us."

"Are you going to see him?"

"When we get back. I won't postpone it."

"That's wonderful, Parker. You'll find it's good to have your parents to talk to."

"So now what?" he asked. "We turn around and go home?"

It had been her thinking from the beginning. She explained, "I was going to have the car shipped back to Chicago, and Lydia I would fly home."

"I don't want to go back. At least not to the life I had," Parker said. He stood up and faced her.

"What do you really want to do? It's your life, Parker. You can do whatever you want."

"Then how about we drive back to Chicago?"

"You're not tired of the road? And me?" McKenna asked.

A gull cawed overhead and they both looked up at it. It swooped into the water and out again.

"I could never be tired of you. And the road has less bumps if I have you along."

A smile spread across her face. "I'm game if you are."

"I have one condition," Parker said.

"What is that?"

"We go back by way of Las Vegas."

"Why Vegas? Neither of us is into gambling."

"I could be. I'm gambling that if I ask you to marry me, we can tie the knot in a small little chapel in the biggest, brashest town on earth."

McKenna stood up straight. "You're not kidding me, are you?"

He shook his head. "It's right there on my bucket list." Opening his hand, he pointed to his palm as if there was a piece of paper with something written on it. "Marry McKenna."

She rushed toward him. Parker reached out and caught her. He steadied her, but didn't let her go. McKenna felt the warmth of him, his strength, his presence. She looked up, intending to say something, but the softness, the kindness in his eyes, that was reflected there, dried her throat. The entire world seemed to change.

The sun shone brighter. The sea swelled. The birds sang. Yet the world around them faded as they were the only inhabitants in the universe.

McKenna tightened her arms around him and accepted the comfort he offered. His mouth found hers in a searing kiss that was undeniable. When he broke contact, he looked at her with a question in his eyes.

"What?" she asked.

"Do you feel guilty that I'm not Marshall? That my kisses are a substitute for his?"

Her arms circled him, feeling they belonged there. "I learned something on this trip." She stared deeply into his eyes. "I loved Marshall with my whole heart. I said goodbye to him at the mountain that morning when you took me there. But I find the heart expands when it needs to. I will always love Marshall. But I love you now, and the love, while the same, is different. It's not something you can explain or put a name to. But when I kiss you, when I tell you I love you, there are no ghosts between us."

Parker kissed her again.

EPILOGUE

WHILE MCKENNA AND Parker had taken months to drive Route 66, they took the highway back to Chicago. They decided not to go to Las Vegas, after all, since Parker wanted his parents to attend the wedding. Detours took them to see Joanna, Sherry and Zeke and they'd invited them to the nuptials once a date was set.

A rousing homecoming welcomed them in the Windy City. McKenna's once-skeptical friends were all assembled and thrilled to hear of the adventures she and Parker had had. Most were slightly jealous of her for acting on a dream, and said they were now considering doing the same. Lydia's leg had healed, although she relied on a cane, which Adrienne whispered was for sympathy only.

Squeals of happiness rose when Parker announced their engagement. Of course, Lydia took full credit for the outcome due to her accident.

Parker realized they should have gone to Las Vegas and married. With the three women all trying to plan a wedding, a circus would surely ensue. But he'd have McKenna and she was worth it.

"Well, what's next for you two?" Lydia asked. "The Cumberland Trail in a covered wagon?"

"As soon as McKenna builds the wagon, we're off," Parker teased.

"The Cumberland Trail," McKenna said, her eyes wandering upward as if she were considering the thought. "A covered wagon. What a great idea. Wouldn't that cause a fight on the way west?" McKenna asked.

Parker caught her and pulled her into his arms. "Only after the honeymoon is over, sweetheart. Only then."

AND...

Joanna Pearson is living with her parents full-time. They went to family counseling and are all doing well. Joanna has a boyfriend who thinks she hung the moon. Her grades continue to be enviable. And she sends email messages to both McKenna and

Parker on a regular basis. She'll be visiting colleges in a year and she plans to check out the University of Chicago. She's considering Economics as a major.

Sherry Granger eventually married 18-wheeler driver Mike. He retired from the road to do construction. Together, they built an addition on to the diner. Her daughter moved to Oklahoma and helps with baking and selling the finished product. The specials of the day always sell out. Sherry took Parker's advice and added a billboard to the highway. It simply reads, Exit Here for Granger's Restaurant, Home Cooked Food at its Best. The dinner hour is always filled to capacity.

And an excited Zeke called McKenna to say thank-you for the rebuilt 1939 engine that arrived shortly after she and Parker reached California. Two months later he'd completed the car's chassis, installed the seats, dashboard lights and fenders. Four months later the car was road ready. He wants McKenna and Parker to return to the small town for a victory ride.

* * * * *

REQUEST YOUR FREE BOOKS!
2 FREE WHOLESOME ROMANCE NOVELS
IN LARGER PRINT
PLUS 2
FREE
MYSTERY GIFTS

☆☆☆☆☆☆☆☆☆☆☆☆☆☆☆☆☆☆☆☆☆☆☆☆☆

HEARTWARMING™

❅❅❅❅❅❅❅❅❅❅❅❅❅❅❅❅❅❅❅❅❅❅❅

Wholesome, tender romances

YES! Please send me 2 FREE Harlequin® Heartwarming Larger-Print novels and my 2 FREE mystery gifts (gifts worth about $10). After receiving them, if I don't wish to receive any more books, I can return the shipping statement marked "cancel." If I don't cancel, I will receive 4 brand-new larger-print novels every month and be billed just $5.24 per book in the U.S. or $5.99 per book in Canada. That's a savings of at least 19% off the cover price. It's quite a bargain! Shipping and handling is just 50¢ per book in the U.S. and 75¢ per book in Canada.* I understand that accepting the 2 free books and gifts places me under no obligation to buy anything. I can always return a shipment and cancel at any time. Even if I never buy another book, the two free books and gifts are mine to keep forever.

161/361 IDN GHX2

Name	(PLEASE PRINT)

Address	Apt. #

City	State/Prov.	Zip/Postal Code

Signature (if under 18, a parent or guardian must sign)

Mail to the **Reader Service:**
IN U.S.A.: P.O. Box 1867, Buffalo, NY 14240-1867
IN CANADA: P.O. Box 609, Fort Erie, Ontario L2A 5X3

* Terms and prices subject to change without notice. Prices do not include applicable taxes. Sales tax applicable in N.Y. Canadian residents will be charged applicable taxes. Offer not valid in Quebec. This offer is limited to one order per household. Not valid for current subscribers to Harlequin Heartwarming larger-print books. All orders subject to credit approval. Credit or debit balances in a customer's account(s) may be offset by any other outstanding balance owed by or to the customer. Please allow 4 to 6 weeks for delivery. Offer available while quantities last.

Your Privacy—The Reader Service is committed to protecting your privacy. Our Privacy Policy is available online at www.ReaderService.com or upon request from the Reader Service.

We make a portion of our mailing list available to reputable third parties that offer products we believe may interest you. If you prefer that we not exchange your name with third parties, or if you wish to clarify or modify your communication preferences, please visit us at www.ReaderService.com/consumerchoice or write to us at Reader Service Preference Service, P.O. Box 9062, Buffalo, NY 14240-9062. Include your complete name and address.

HW15

LARGER-PRINT BOOKS!

GET 2 FREE LARGER-PRINT NOVELS PLUS 2 FREE MYSTERY GIFTS

Love Inspired®

Larger-print novels are now available...

YES! Please send me 2 FREE LARGER-PRINT Love Inspired® novels and my 2 FREE mystery gifts (gifts are worth about $10). After receiving them, if I don't wish to receive any more books, I can return the shipping statement marked "cancel." If I don't cancel, I will receive 6 brand-new novels every month and be billed just $5.49 per book in the U.S. or $5.99 per book in Canada. That's a savings of at least 19% off the cover price. It's quite a bargain! Shipping and handling is just 50¢ per book in the U.S. and 75¢ per book in Canada.* I understand that accepting the 2 free books and gifts places me under no obligation to buy anything. I can always return a shipment and cancel at any time. Even if I never buy another book, the two free books and gifts are mine to keep forever.

122/322 IDN GH6D

Name	(PLEASE PRINT)
Address	Apt. #
City	State/Prov.	Zip/Postal Code

Signature (if under 18, a parent or guardian must sign)

Mail to the **Reader Service:**
IN U.S.A.: P.O. Box 1867, Buffalo, NY 14240-1867
IN CANADA: P.O. Box 609, Fort Erie, Ontario L2A 5X3

**Are you a current subscriber to Love Inspired® books
and want to receive the larger-print edition?
Call 1-800-873-8635 or visit www.ReaderService.com.**

* Terms and prices subject to change without notice. Prices do not include applicable taxes. Sales tax applicable in N.Y. Canadian residents will be charged applicable taxes. Offer not valid in Quebec. This offer is limited to one order per household. Not valid to current subscribers to Love Inspired Larger-Print books. All orders subject to credit approval. Credit or debit balances in a customer's account(s) may be offset by any other outstanding balance owed by or to the customer. Please allow 4 to 6 weeks for delivery. Offer available while quantities last.

Your Privacy—The Reader Service is committed to protecting your privacy. Our Privacy Policy is available online at www.ReaderService.com or upon request from the Reader Service.

We make a portion of our mailing list available to reputable third parties that offer products we believe may interest you. If you prefer that we not exchange your name with third parties, or if you wish to clarify or modify your communication preferences, please visit us at www.ReaderService.com/consumerschoice or write to us at Reader Service Preference Service, P.O. Box 9062, Buffalo, NY 14240-9062. Include your complete name and address.

LILP15

READERSERVICE.COM

Manage your account online!
- Review your order history
- Manage your payments
- Update your address

> ### We've designed the Reader Service website just for you.

Enjoy all the features!
- Discover new series available to you, and read excerpts from any series.
- Respond to mailings and special monthly offers.
- Connect with favorite authors at the blog.
- Browse the Bonus Bucks catalog and online-only exculsives.
- Share your feedback.

Visit us at:
ReaderService.com